W.i.t.c.h

Will   Irma   Taranee   Cornelia   Hay Lin

The Darkest Dream

Adapted by KATE EGAN

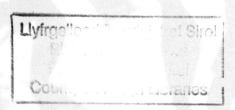

This book was first published in the USA in 2004 by Volo/Hyperion Books for Children
First published in Great Britain in 2006 by HarperCollins *Children's Books*, a division of
HarperCollins Publishers Ltd.

© 2006 Disney Enterprises, Inc.

ISBN 0-00-720953-3
ISBN13 978-0-00-720953-8

1 3 5 7 9 10 8 6 4 2

The HarperCollins website is:
www.harpercollinschildrensbooks.co.uk

Visit www.clubwitch.co.uk

Printed and bound in Italy

SEE W.I.T.C.H. #16.

ONE

Well, this is it, Will thought. The end of our vacation.

She sighed as she climbed into Cornelia's car. Cornelia's dad would be driving both Will and Cornelia back home to Heatherfield, and then Will would be leaving on another vacation – this one with her mum.

That trip sure won't be like this one, Will thought, sighing again. It won't be half as much fun without all my friends.

Irma was standing with her family outside their cabin, waving goodbye. Will waved back and fumbled for her seat belt before she closed the door. She couldn't help hearing what Irma's little brother, Christopher, was saying. "And so?" he teased Irma.

"That's all? What about the tears? Girls always cry when they say goodbye!"

As usual, Irma had a snappy comeback. "Since when do you understand girls?" she asked her brother.

"Girls always cry when they do stuff like this on TV!" Christopher claimed.

Irma crossed her arms and gave him a quasi-patient smile. "Well, clearly, normal girls aren't on the TV shows you watch!" she replied.

Leave it to Irma, Will thought, smiling as she slammed the car door shut. There's nothing to cry about, she reminded herself, no matter what Christopher says! I hate to be leaving, but this has been the best vacation ever.

For the past week, Will and her four best friends had been bonding, big-time, at Irma's beach house. The place was tiny and crowded, but nobody cared about the cramped quarters. The sun was shining. The beach was just steps away. And all of them were together again . . . at last.

Will hadn't known Irma, Cornelia, Hay Lin, and Taranee for very long. But they'd been through a lot in a really short time. They'd traded gossip, shared secrets, and confessed their crushes. They'd played games, gone to parties, and had sleepovers. They'd survived a school year. And, oh, yeah . . . they'd also saved the world.

Talk about bonding! It had all started way back when Will and Taranee had both been the newbies in town. They'd met Irma, Hay Lin, and Cornelia in school, and soon they were all practically joined at the hip. They thought they'd had a lot in common . . . even before they discovered the one thing that would tie them together forever.

They got that news one afternoon while they were relaxing in the apartment above Hay Lin's family's restaurant. Hay Lin's grandmother was the one to tell the girls that they had been brought together in Heatherfield for a very important job. The five had been chosen as the new Guardians of the Veil. And even freakier – Hay Lin's grandmother had been one before them! A benevolent and all-knowing being called the Oracle had anointed them. He lived in a distant and ethereal world called Candracar, suspended someplace between time and infinity. From there, we kept watch. The

Oracle had high hopes for the girls – after all, they had a tough mission ahead.

Many centuries before, the Oracle had erected the Veil – an invisible barrier designed to protect the peaceful earth from a dark and turbulent land called Metamoor. With the coming of the new millennium, though, cosmic forces had begun to wear the Veil down. Now portals were beginning to pop up all over it – and the Oracle feared that evil beings from Metamoor could use these openings to sneak to the earth and cause trouble!

The Oracle needed his Guardians to close the portals and keep the bad guys out. To help them complete this task, Guardians had special and unique powers. Four of the girls had control over one of the elements of nature. Irma's power flowed through water. Solid Cornelia had power over the earth, while Hay Lin's power was as light as air. And quiet Taranee had a way with fire.

Where did this leave Will? She had been given the strangest power of them all. She had power over energy and she was the Keeper of the Heart of Candracar, a sparkling pink orb nestled in a silver clasp that popped into the palm of her hand whenever she needed it most. When she summoned the Heart, Will and her friends turned into stronger versions of them-selves – in clothes to die for. The Heart drew the other four powers together and multiplied their force. When the girls' powers were joined in the Heart, they could handle whatever came their way. That also meant that Will had been made the unofficial leader of their group.

Even as Will and her friends were fighting dark forces, Cornelia had managed to fall in love. Cornelia had no problem meeting boys. But this time, it was totally different. This wasn't just some average guy. Cornelia had had dreams about this boy for a long time before she actu-ally met him face-to-face. Then, suddenly, there he was . . . right in the middle of all the trouble in Metamoor. The odds were totally against them, but it was love at first sight.

The boy's name was Caleb, and once, he'd been one of Prince Phobos's Murmurers, a captive who had been turned into a flower and then trapped in the prince's expansive gardens. The Murmurers were Phobos's spies, his eyes and ears within the kingdom that he ruled unmercifully. But through the sheer force of his own will, Caleb had escaped his viny existence. He turned back into a boy first, and then became the leader of the rebellion against the prince! The only sign that he had been a plant was the presence of two green marks on his cheeks.

The connection between Cornelia and Caleb soon became a connection between the Guardians and the rebels.

The Guardians had saved Metamoor, returned Elyon – the rightful heir – to the throne, fulfilled the Oracle's prophecies, and restored order to the universe. They were proud of all they'd accomplished. But the price had been high. Things weren't good when they returned back home, because Cornelia was devastated. Prince Phobos had cruelly changed Caleb back into a flower. After that, Cornelia kept Caleb in a vase, and spent all of her time at home alone with him.

I thought it was pretty crazy at the time, Will remembered. But now I guess I can see how she felt. Love hurts.

Without Cornelia, there really wasn't any W.I.T.C.H. (That was the name they'd given themselves – the word was an acronym using the first letter of each girl's name.) Soon, the other girls began arguing among themselves. And since the key to their power lay in their friendship, their magic quickly sputtered out as well.

Their power was restored when they stopped arguing. Once again, they had the Power of Five.

Will was jolted from her thoughts by the honk of the horn. The car in front of them held Taranee and her family, heading to a town called Sesamo way up in the mountains; Mr. Hale beeped when he turned off in the other direction.

Will felt a pang. She wasn't sure when she'd see Taranee next. The girls were all heading their separate ways for now.

Mr. Hale turned to face Will and his daughter in the backseat. "This is your captain speaking!" he announced, trying to sound serious. "Please lock your tray tables and restore your seats to their full and upright positions."

Cornelia rolled her eyes, as if to say, "He's so corny!" But Will didn't mind a few bad jokes. The car trip with Cornelia and Mr. Hale would probably be better than a car trip with her mum.

Will and her mum had been getting along a little better lately, but nothing between them was ever easy – especially road trips! Will liked Mr. Hale's easygoing nature.

Mr. Hale leaned forward and popped a CD in the car's CD player. "You girls don't mind if I put on a little of my music, do you?" he asked.

Cornelia shrugged and looked at Will.

"Go right ahead, Mr. Hale," Will piped up.

It can't be any worse than the *Action Hero* theme song Irma's brother has been singing all week, she thought.

But it was. It was opera. And to top it off, Mr. Hale began singing along! Will didn't know the song, but she was pretty sure it wasn't supposed to sound like that. "*La ci darem la manoo!*" Mr. Hale wailed. "*Le ci darem di siii . . .*"

Is it supposed to be another language, or does it just sound that way? Will wondered.

She wriggled around trying to get comfortable. There was no way to talk above the singing, so Will went back to reviewing her vacation in her mind. And Matt. She shivered for a moment just thinking about the text messages she'd been getting from her crush since the moment they'd arrived.

It's crazy! We've only had one real date, Will marvelled. *But I feel like I'm getting to know him so well! Somehow it just seems right.*

Will wasn't an expert on boys, so this was all new to her.

Will we ever be boyfriend and girlfriend? Will wondered. *My friends are all telling me just to go for it. But look at what happened to Cornelia and Caleb! They seemed so in love and so happy. Then it all just fell apart. I don't think I could deal with that. What if Matt gets in the way of W.I.T.C.H.? What if he discovers who I really am and flips out? And what if he keeps me from preparing for our next mission . . . whatever it is?*

Will and her friends didn't know exactly what they were going to be up against next. But strange things were already starting to happen. For one thing, a big, armoured monster seemed to be stalking the girls, and they'd ended up having a big showdown with him on the beach one night during their vacation. They'd combined their magic to take away the pair of deadly axes he was swinging at them.

But the thug disappeared before we could finish him off, Will remembered. *We don't really* know where he went, but he's got to be connected with Nerissa somehow. That's why he wears her symbol on his chest.

Nerissa. Will was still trying to keep *that* story straight in her mind.

Nerissa was a Guardian of the Veil long ago, Will reminded herself. And she was just like me – the Keeper of the Heart – before something went terribly wrong. She tried to steal the Heart for herself and use it for wrong instead of right. The other Guardians – including Hay Lin's grandmother – tried to stop her, but Nerissa was consumed and corrupted by the Heart's intense power. She fought ferociously. She would stop at nothing to keep the Heart to herself – which is why she ended up killing another Guardian, a girl named Cassidy.

Will knew that the Oracle had punished Nerissa severely. Nerissa was sentenced to exile in desolate Mount Thanos, where all of the elements melded together as one. There, she was sealed up in a tomb of stone. She would have all of eternity to contemplate her crime, since she would only be set free in the remote event the five Guardians' powers were ever united. And *that* would never happen. Or, it was never *supposed to* . . .

. . . But it did . . .

. . . And now, Will thought with a shudder, we have to be on guard, because she says she's coming to get us!

In Candracar, Hay Lin's grandmother had told the girls what they could expect.

What were her words again? Will wondered. Oh, yeah . . . *"The enemy you have before you is terrible and heartless."* "Heartless" was a good way to put it. After all, that enemy wanted to take the Heart away from Will.

The good news was that Will and her friends were up to the challenge. No doubt about it after this week, she thought, glowing. We're back and better than ever. We're ready to take on any task . . . together.

But still, Will was a little worried about the emergency plan Irma had concocted. She wanted them to use astral drops in case of an emergency.

But using astral drops always seemed to get us in trouble, Will thought. Let's hope we don't have to use them.

There was another problem, too. If some kind of crisis came up, Will wanted to rise to the occasion. But there was no getting around it: she was wiped out. She hadn't had any good sleep in days, because every time she drifted off, she heard a quavery voice whispering in her ear. Nerissa's voice!

Nerissa came to me in a nightmare, Will remembered, the first day at Irma's. Somehow, even in my dream, she tried to drag me underwater! She had such power. Why can't she leave me alone? My friends are going to think I'm losing my mind. But I've got to tell someone or I am *really* going to lose it.

She glanced over at Cornelia, who was gazing out the window. I hate to dump this on her, Will thought. She has enough on her mind already.

"My dad probably can't get over the fact that someone agreed to listen to his opera blasting at stomach-churning volume!" Cornelia joked.

Will gulped. "Well, the louder the better!" she said in a low whisper. "That way he won't hear what I'm about to tell you." Will put her arm across the back of the seat and inched closer to her friend. "Before getting everyone worried, I wanted to get your opinion. Maybe it's just my imagination, but I think I'm hearing a voice when I'm half asleep! A sort of creepy whisper!"

She switched back to her normal voice to explain the rest. There was no way Mr. Hale would hear her over his bad singing, and she wanted to be sure Cornelia didn't miss a word. "I think it's that old Guardian that Hay Lin's grandmother was talking about!"

Cornelia looked concerned. "Nerissa?" she asked.

"Yeah, her!" Will confirmed. She took a deep breath. It felt good finally to get this off her chest. "She keeps threatening me and demanding the Heart of Candracar! But why? I mean, I never asked to be the Keeper in the first place!" Suddenly, she felt overwhelmed. She hated to admit it, but she was feeling a little sorry for herself.

But apparently Cornelia had no time for the little self-pity party. There was a reason she had power over the earth – the girl was totally grounded. "Will, by saying that, you're playing right into her hands," Cornelia said.

Cornelia's right, Will thought. But enough of this already! I'm so tired!

She wrapped her arms around herself and yawned. "All I know is that I don't want to hear her voice anymore, Cornelia! It's getting to the point where I hardly want to shut my eyes!"

Of course, Cornelia had some advice. "Just think of something else before you go to sleep," she suggested gently. "Like Matt, for instance."

Will wondered if Cornelia could guess that she thought about Matt all the time – awake or asleep, it didn't matter. She didn't want anyone to know she'd fallen so hard for him so fast, and she was trying to play it cool. "Yeah, him!" Will shrugged. "He's probably already forgotten about me!"

Will closed her eyes. She could see his face in her mind. His dazzling smile and his adorable, floppy hair. She loved the way he dressed and the way his voice soared when he sang with his band. "It feels like he's so far away," she allowed herself to say, opening her eyes. "I wish I could meet the genius who said that absence makes the heart grow fonder!"

Cornelia's eyes suddenly welled up with tears.

Uh-oh, thought Will. What did I say?

"Whoever it was," Cornelia whispered,

"they definitely were never in love, you know. Love is kind of like a rare disease . . ."

Cornelia wasn't actually crying, but her voice was shaking, and the tears were flooding her eyes so that Will wondered how she could see. Will was admiring her friend's awesome self-control when Cornelia totally lost it.

". . . You only recognise it once you've caught the symptoms," Cornelia finished. She covered her face with her hands.

Why'd I have to go and mention love? Will wondered. I should have known Cornelia would get upset. First Caleb is turned into a flower. And then, when Cornelia manages to bring him back to boy form, she gets in trouble for it. And now, Caleb is alive and well – but stuck in Candracar. Forever. I've been up all night with Nerissa haunting me, Will thought. But, talk about tired. This thing with Caleb is one long nightmare for Cornelia!

Cornelia and Will hadn't always seen eye to eye. Cornelia could be a little bossy, while Will was *supposed* to be the boss – even if she didn't always like it.

Who'd have thought boys would be what brought us together? Will mused. I don't really understand how she feels about Caleb, but I now have an inkling. I'd flip out if I knew I wouldn't see Matt again for a long time! And here she is, trying to act like everything's normal. She's even stronger than I thought.

Will was mortified that she'd brought up a subject that hurt her friend.

That'll teach you to think twice before you open your mouth, she ordered herself sternly. But if there's one thing I remember after the week at Irma's, it's how important it is that we stick together. We're still repairing some major damage, and we can't let anything – or anyone – separate us ever again.

Will wrapped her arms around Cornelia in a tight bear hug.

"Sorry!" sputtered Cornelia.

"No, I'm sorry!" Will apologised over and over. "I'm so dumb."

She thought for a minute and then had an idea that she hoped might help them both. "Give me your hand, Cornelia," she said, searching for it. "If you hold it tight, maybe this time I'll finally manage to close my eyes!"

TWO

Since the moment of Nerissa's sentencing, stars had been born and died, suns had risen and set, countless years had begun and ended. The universe had expanded, and time had marched on. Within Mount Thanos, however, little had changed.

The thick walls of Nerissa's tomb were engraved with an ancient language, recounting her cautionary tale. Protective spells were etched among the stories, to keep Nerissa in her place. Time had done nothing to erode the appearance or the meaning of the spells, nothing to alter the facts of Nerissa's history, and nothing to extinguish Nerissa's fury.

It had been many centuries

since Nerissa had entered the tomb. Volcanic fires danced incessantly outside, but inside Nerissa lay still, contained and constrained by the heavy stone and the potent magic surrounding her on all four sides.

I may have been motionless, Nerissa thought, but only a fool would say I was at rest! The Oracle and his Congregation thought I would repent for my mistakes in this barren place. Instead, I have been waiting for my revenge!

Nerissa had never been distracted by the hypnotic hiss of the flames that engulfed her. She kept focused on her scheme and disregarded everything around her. But even she had been surprised on the day a colossal blast had blown the top off her tomb. My time has come! she had thought. But she did not know why. At least, she did not know back then.

Since that moment, Nerissa had flexed her flaccid muscles to restore their strength. Then she had willed herself to stand – and failed. That had not stopped her from beginning to put her plan into place.

Nothing, she gloated, could prevent me from seeking what is rightfully mine! The Heart!

But her weakness had nagged Nerissa. She could not help wondering: how shall I win back the Heart if I am stiff and bent? I may have been trapped here against my will for longer than I know. But I am no old woman!

Now something extraordinary had happened. It delighted her like nothing else she could remember, and the elation delivered to her a burst of new strength. Nerissa had crept inside the Keeper's mind to plant the seeds of fear and doubt. She was also learning a great deal about this new Keeper of the Heart. This Guardian had quite a story to tell. Nerissa was intrigued.

I shall use this information to my best advantage, she reveled. It shall be the key to my triumph!

Nerissa clutched the sides of the tomb with her bony fingers, her nails long and twisted from centuries of neglect. She was filled with purpose and certainty. She could do it, she felt. This was the time. Nerissa closed her eyes and, thin arms quivering, hoisted herself to the top of the tomb. When she cleared the edge, she opened her eyes and gazed upon her surroundings for the first time since the Oracle had proclaimed her punishment so long ago. Below her was the swirling lava of the volcano. She was in a cave. It all looked beautiful to Nerissa. She allowed a wave of pleasure to wash over her.

I am one step closer to the goal, she realised. I am one step closer to the Heart.

Nerissa leaned out of the tomb, her long hair tumbling over its wall in filthy waves. She pulled out her trusty staff, and her lips contorted in a smile, exposing her broken and rotten teeth. She could see Khor, her terrifying henchman, standing guard beside the tomb. Nerissa announced her presence and her glorious news. "Ahhh!" she roared. "Great news from the world of nightmares!"

Khor stared at her stupidly and growled "Rrrrr!"

Is that all he can say? Nerissa grimaced. At a moment like this? I will have to spell it out for him, I suppose.

Nerissa addressed him directly. "Well, beast of destruction, Nerissa is once again strong enough to stand. Today she might even laugh from the heart . . . if she had one, that is!" Nerissa burst into hysterical laughter.

Khor watched her mutely, his massive

arms clasped behind his back.

Nerissa did not like what she saw. "What is it, Khor? Is that a grimace of fear contorting your repulsive face?" she demanded. The dog! she fumed. The dumb dog!

When Nerissa's tomb had first been torn in two, she was quick to notice a figure cowering on the edge of the volcano. She did not care who it was. Nerissa knew that she would make this being her servant, as help would be difficult to find in this isolated outpost. Nerissa would have preferred a human servant, but destiny had brought her only a dog. She had transformed him utterly with her angry magic.

Khor had the sinew and muscle of the creature he'd once been, the quick reflexes and the sharp teeth of a canine, all in the body of a giant man. His fearsome armor was emblazoned with Nerissa's ominous symbol. Khor wasn't much company, however, Nerissa realised. This thought sent her into gales of mirth.

Really, she thought, shaking herself. I must explain my good fortune to this dolt!

Nerissa swung her staff further than she had in hundreds, perhaps thousands of years. The end of it was twisted into the shape of her mark, and after all this time it still did her bidding with the utmost speed. With a mighty *kraak!* it yanked some red-hot flames together and created a kind of looking glass. Nerissa would use it to show Khor what the Guardians had shown her in their dreams.

"Once again I've managed to enter the dreams of the young Keeper of the Heart of Candracar!" Nerissa began, with great ceremony. "Yet this time Will was not alone! One of her friends was holding her hand!" The blonde one, Nerissa thought; they were in a car, and she was crying. "So I explored their thoughts!" Nerissa crowed. "I crept into their world!"

Nerissa showed Khor an image of the girls' hands in the flaming mirror. "Between dreams and memories," she told Khor, "I saw those who condemned me! The Oracle and his worthy followers!" The wretches, Nerissa added to herself. Worthy of what?

She conjured the picture so Khor could see their hateful faces gathered in a meeting of their Council. The Elders sat on benches lining a round room that glittered with the reflection of a million crystals. At the centre of the room was the detested Oracle, gazing somberly at a cat-woman. It was Luba, the Keeper of the Aurameres. But the people on trial this time were the Guardians! Nerissa observed the proceedings just as Cornelia remembered them.

Luba made her case against the Guardians with great passion. They had always been too self-centered and immature for their task, Luba argued. Yes, they had closed the portals, but their good luck would not last if they continued to show such poor judgment.

They were weak. For example, Luba said, the Council should consider Cornelia. Unusual circumstances had united in her all five of the great powers at once: those of earth and air, fire, water, energy – not to mention the Heart of Candracar. And what had Cornelia done? She had used those powers to revive a Murmurer! The girl believed herself in love with him, but Luba reminded the gathering that any Murmurer would remain Phobos's servant for eternity. The girl was in love with their enemy. Cornelia had put herself, the other Guardians, and Candracar in danger.

There was only one way to handle this irresponsible child and her cohorts, Luba concluded. Declare Khandran!

Nerissa remembered all too well what that was: the sentencing of the Guardians and their replacement. Does Khor follow me so far? Nerissa wondered. I must spell it out for him as clearly as I can. Recapping, she said, "I discovered that Luba, the Keeper of the Aurameres, is convinced the Chosen Ones are unfit and unworthy!" Khor nodded, so Nerissa raced on to the dramatic conclusion. "Then, most importantly, I saw Caleb! Cornelia's one true love!" she said, sneering. "He is the Herald of Candracar!" Nerissa stared intently into the flames. And my key to the Guardians' downfall, she added silently.

What happened next was still almost too shocking for her to grasp.

Luba's diatribe was over, but the Oracle did not look convinced. If anything, Nerissa realised, he looked sympathetic. A sentiment he never showed to me! she seethed. He seemed to agree that Cornelia's behaviour demanded consequences, but he also seemed to think it was an accident. He appeared to be mulling it over when a young man approached him. The young man had longish hair and piercing blue eyes. This was the Murmurer in question, in the form of a boy. His name was Caleb.

Cornelia's eyes never wavered from Caleb as he spoke respectfully to the Oracle.

"If Cornelia made a mistake," he said, "it was all my fault! And that is why I ask that she be given her power back!" Luba attempted to silence him, but Caleb was persistent. "Punish me, not Cornelia!" he begged.

The Oracle was listening. And so was Nerissa. "I can give Cornelia back her power," Caleb explained. "The power she used to bring *me* back! And in exchange – if the Council will allow me to do so – I will remain in the Temple as your servant!"

The scene in the flames faded, and only Caleb's image was visible. Nerissa ran through the sequence again in her mind. For some reason the girl had all five powers at her fingertips. She had used those powers to revive the boy. Whatever he gives to his girlfriend now, Nerissa noted, the powers will *still* reside in the boy. And now *he* resides in Candracar – where I know how to get him!

Nerissa snickered. Then she pulled herself together and finished the story for Khor.

"Although it may seem astonishing, I will owe my second life to this young man!" she proclaimed. "I still remember the Oracle's prophetic words just after my sentencing!" Nerissa's eyes narrowed with the memory. "He said, 'The day on which the five powers live in a single person, you will return to life.'"

The universe had stopped when the powers were united in Cornelia – and Nerissa had been freed! Then Cornelia had transferred the powers to Caleb. Through him, now, Nerissa would engineer the destruction of them all! The words echoed in Nerissa's mind: return to life. Return to life. And return to the Heart! she vowed.

"Yes, beast!" she screeched. "Within him, Caleb holds a copy of the Guardians' five powers. It is thanks to him that I am free once more! And it will be thanks to him that Candracar will fall! My revenge knows no haste, faithful Khor. But when it rages down against the temple, it will be fierce, inexorable, and final!" Nerissa glared defiantly and shook her fist at the beast to punctuate her point.

Then she took Khor's dreadful face in her hands. "Your new mission will be to take me to Caleb!" she said softly. "But for this task you must have help!" Nerissa raised her staff to the sky and screeched, "You will need desperation! The same sense of anger I felt, locked up within this prison of ice and fire!" Sparks flew around Nerissa's staff as her voice reached a pitch that only a dog could have heard. Then particles of ice began to fly toward the staff, attracted by the magnetic force of Nerissa's evil magic. *Fraatch!* The ice-cold particles fused together and formed the shape of a winged strongman in steely armor.

Nerissa continued her incantation. "You will need pain – what they will be sure to feel in Candracar when my fiery rage destroys the Temple!" *Blooarp!* Bursts of lava sprang from the volcano beneath and took the shape of a dangerously beautiful woman, armed with a deadly spear and a smoldering, red-eyed gaze.

"And finally," Nerissa screamed, "you will be accompanied by the most powerful emotion of all: hate!" She stopped for a moment. "For this, I must start with something more versatile than ice and magma." But then, as if on cue, Nerissa spotted a lonely figure on the desolate snowscape beyond Mount Thanos. He was the owner of the dog that Khor had been, a geologist studying this last frontier of frozen wilderness.

His voice echoed over the ice. "Miska!" he called. There was a desperate note in the sound. "Miska!"

Nerissa drew a deep breath of satisfaction. "Ahh," she said. "Here is the raw material, just in time: it is a man, Khor!"

Khor stared blankly at her, awaiting a command. Nerissa's yellow eyes lit up. "It is you he seeks," she announced to Khor. "Before you met me, you were Miska – his faithful little dog."

Khor had nothing to say but "Urrrrh!"

Nerissa cackled. "Yes! This man will become the perfect servant for revenge!" She reached for her neck and drew a chain from under her tattered purple robes. At the end of the chain hung a pendant, a tarnished silver replica of her sign. Nerissa stared at it as she swung it back and forth.

"My much-awaited revenge," she whispered. The pendant moved from east to west, from north to south, Nerissa's eyes following it until she was transfixed by the motion and her deepest power was released.

Mount Thanos went completely silent. The

ice stopped creaking, the lava stopped gurgling, and the wind stopped whistling. Suddenly, a primal howl escaped Nerissa's throat. "My revenge!" she shrieked. Light as bright and as harsh as the sound poured through the lightning bolt at the centre of Nerissa's necklace.

Roooumble! The lake of lava inside the volcano rippled and trembled with the force of Nerissa's rage.

Nerissa's vision was sharper and clearer when she was mesmerized by magic. She could see past and present. She could see near and far. She could see the Oracle meditating in his Temple. She could see the Guardians hurtling down a highway in a car. She could see geologists, the friends of Miska's master, carefully recording the tremors she had caused.

Soon, she vowed, they shall all see *me*. And they shall know my wrath!

THREE

I wish Dad would turn down the air-conditioning, Cornelia thought, hugging herself with her bare arms. It's freezing in here! Suddenly, though, it seemed too much of an effort to say anything. Cornelia was exhausted and felt herself drifting off. She leaned her head against the backseat window and closed her eyes. Soon her body was relaxed and her breathing was regular. The blonde Guardian was asleep, or as close to it as she could get.

Cornelia could feel the headlong rush of the car down the highway. She could sense her father's breakneck pace with every bump and turn the car took in the road. But she was also conscious of something else, which she couldn't quite place. It was a sort of rumble in the distance. A quiet roar.

Somewhere in the back of her mind, Cornelia was still alert. You're supposed to clear your brain before you go to sleep, she thought. But it feels like somebody is trying to do that for me.

The persistent whine reminded her of a vacuum cleaner, sucking up whatever was in its way. Her thoughts. Her memories. Her secrets.

Suddenly there was a hand on her elbow and a voice exclaiming, "Cornelia!" Cornelia's heart leaped in her throat, and her arms flailed to attack whoever was after her.

Her eyes flew open. It was only Will. "Wake up, Cornelia!" her friend said cheerfully.

"Will! Oh, Will!" She'd been shivering just seconds before, and now, despite the chill in the car, she was drenched in sweat.

That was a horrible nightmare, she thought with a shudder.

Cornelia realised she must look like a mess. Will looked at her quizzically, and then said softly, "Shhh! The opera's over." When she was sure Mr. Hale wasn't paying attention, she added, "You had a nightmare, too, didn't you?"

Cornelia knew it wasn't really a question.

She slowly nodded. Poor Will! Cornelia suddenly thought. She's been having these nightmares for *a week*! She must be exhausted. I would be. How weird that it's Will, of all people, that I can turn to now!

Cornelia still remembered meeting Will for the first time. Cornelia was one of the Infielders – the cool crowd at Sheffield Institute – and she knew that, with her rumpled hair and her air of uncertainty, Will wasn't.

I was wrong, though, Cornelia admitted to herself. Ever since the disaster with Caleb, it was a little easier for Cornelia to own up to her mistakes. Now that something this huge had happened, she wasn't bothering to sweat the small stuff.

Who'd have guessed that Will and I would be finding so much common ground? Cornelia mused. Who'd have guessed I'd ever share my *dreams* with her? I used to turn to Elyon for that, but now that she is the queen of Meridian, I don't think she has the time to deal with my sleeping habits. Will is the only one who can relate to my Nerissa nightmare. Plus, with Matt in the picture, she can really understand the way Caleb has stolen my heart. I had problems with her before. But now I'd follow her anywhere.

Cornelia felt Will's questioning gaze on her. She knew she should say something, so she tried to describe how the dream had felt. "I don't remember any of the details," she told Will, "but I still have this strange sensation. . . ."

"It felt like somebody had squeezed all the air out of my lungs!" Will said, referring to her own nightmare.

"That's it! Exactly!" Cornelia cried. "So you think Nerissa . . ."

"You'll have to leave your little secrets for another time, girls!" said Cornelia's dad, cutting her off. He looked at them in the rearview mirror. "We're here!"

Mr. Hale pulled up outside their apartment building. Will's mum was waiting in her red car. When she saw them arrive, she jumped out and approached Will with open arms.

That's a change, Cornelia noted. For the better. It wasn't so long ago that the two of them were constantly bickering.

"Hi, honey!" Mrs. Vandom exclaimed. "You

look beautiful! Even if I can tell that you went *shade*-bathing as usual!"

"Hi, Mum," muttered Will. "I . . . I didn't have much time to sit in the sun!"

Cornelia cringed. No time . . . on her vacation? Will still had a thing or two to learn about the quick and witty comeback.

Mrs. Vandom didn't seem to notice that her daughter wasn't making any sense, nor being superfriendly. She was too busy talking to Cornelia's dad. "Something came up at the office, as usual. Thank you so much for giving Will a ride!"

Mr. Hale smiled graciously. "It was no problem. She was an angel for the whole trip!" He winked at Will and added, "Plus, I found out that Mozart's *Don Giovanni* puts her right to sleep!"

While their parents were making small talk, Cornelia climbed out of the car and opened the trunk. She lifted out a couple of bags and handed them to Will.

I don't want her to go, Cornelia realised suddenly. Not with Nerissa still sneaking around our dreams. We are stronger together.

Cornelia wondered if Will was thinking

about the same thing. But Will wasn't saying much of anything at that moment.

"Um, well, see you around, Cornelia," she said awkwardly, looking down at her feet.

Cornelia's mind was racing. It felt as if time were running out.

What if we have to find each other while we're apart? she wondered. Will's leaving on this trip with her mum, and I'm going with my family to the lake. Hay Lin and Irma are still at the beach, Taranee is in the mountains, and the only way we have of getting in touch is some crazy idea that Irma dreamed up!

"I hate to admit it, but I think maybe Irma was right!" she whispered into Will's ear. She couldn't believe that she was actually agreeing with Irma. That never happened!

I guess desperate times call for desperate measures, Cornelia thought.

Out loud, she added, "I mean, the plan's not perfect. To say the least. But we might need to see each other sooner than we think."

Will gave her friend a goodbye hug. "Got it!" she said. She looked over her shoulder and noticed that the adults had grown silent. "Well . . . let's keep in touch," she said blandly. "And remember Irma's Operation E.G.A.D."

Cornelia felt a pang of sadness as she watched the Vandoms pull away.

First Caleb left me, she thought, and now all my friends have gone, too. I need to get a grip. I know Caleb loves me. I know my friends are here for me. They've been here for me all along – even when I was holed up in my room, crying over a flower. So why do I feel so alone? What's happening to me? I used to be totally independent, but now I'm all needy. I feel like I don't even know myself anymore!

Her dad's voice cut in to her thoughts. "Let's get going, Blondie," he called out. "Our real trip hasn't even begun!"

Her dad headed in to the lobby of their building, and Cornelia followed behind. While they waited for the elevator, she asked, "Can't we leave tomorrow, too, like Will and her mum?" She thought she could really use a long, hot bath before the trip with her family.

"Nope! Riddlescott Lake is waiting for us," her dad replied briskly. "And we have to give a ride to . . . a certain someone."

What is he talking about? Cornelia wondered. My dad can be so weird!

But at least she was prepared for a surprise when the door to her family's apartment opened. What she wasn't prepared for was to be just about knocked over by a cloud of cheap perfume in the living room. Then she heard the most grating, nasal voice.

"Daaahling!" the voice said. "Let me take a look at you! What gorgeous hair! And you have your mother's eyes! Bet she never told you about me!"

Cornelia turned to see a woman sitting on the blue sofa across from her mum. "I'm Sandra!" the woman said. "Sandra Doubman! I was your mum's best friend in high school. We were inseparable! Practically sisters!"

Cornelia had never heard of her. And what is she wearing, she wondered? Sandra had a gold ring on almost every finger and massive gold earrings dangling to her shoulders. Her long, dark hair was slicked into place by about two tubes of styling gel, Cornelia estimated. And it looked as if she'd found her sleeveless shirt in the deep-discount section of a department store.

Mum must have met her before she learned good taste, Cornelia decided. If her mum was surprised by Sandra's strange appearance, though, she didn't let on. "Sandra and I ran into each other yesterday . . ." Mrs. Hale said, shooting Cornelia a warning look.

"By pure chance!" Sandra interrupted. "Isn't that funny? I walked into her studio and I just about fainted! 'You? Here?' I said. . . ."

Cornelia tried not to roll her eyes as Sandra shared every detail of their meeting. ". . . And she recognised me right away, of course! I haven't changed a bit, what with all I spend at the beauty parlor . . ."

Walking around the couch, Cornelia's dad looked quizzically at Sandra from several different angles. It almost seemed as if he didn't believe Sandra was real. She sure seemed like a faker to Cornelia.

"Harold! What on earth are you doing?" Cornelia's mum asked Mr. Hale in a frustrated tone.

"Nothing, Elizabeth," he said quickly. "Just looking for something."

Sandra didn't seem to notice the tension. ". . . It's just a matter of complexion, you know!" she droned on. "I wage war against wrinkles, and I follow a special exercise regimen. For instance, there's one that . . ."

Just when Cornelia thought she couldn't take it anymore, her dad sidled up and spoke to her softly. "No luck!" he said. "I couldn't find a cord! I think she runs on batteries!"

Cornelia smothered a giggle and sped out of the room. At least one of my parents will think it's ok if I go upstairs, she decided. Dad probably wants to leave, too.

But the coast wasn't clear up there, either. Cornelia's little sister, Lilian, stood in the hallway, holding something behind her back. It was Cornelia's hairbrush. "Why were you and Daddy laughing downstairs?" she demanded. "Can you tell me, too?"

Cornelia snapped, "No, you little pest! And you're in for it if you took my hairbrush!"

"Oh, man," whined Lilian. "Couldn't you have stayed at the beach a couple more months?"

I should probably calm down, Cornelia thought. Lilian didn't do anything to me. At least, not today. *And* she's been stuck here with Sandra Doubman. "Yeah," Cornelia said lightly. "But I decided to come back here just to be mean to you. By the way, have you seen

Napoleon?" she added.

With an annoyed look at her sister, Lilian pointed to her closed bedroom door.

Napoleon was the cat Will had given Cornelia after she had come back from Metamoor and Caleb had been changed into a flower. Cornelia wasn't exactly grateful for the gift at first – she'd been too wrapped up in her heartbreak for that. But later, Napoleon had saved Caleb when a crow flew through the window and tried to eat the boy's petals. She and Napoleon became friends after that.

The black cat was the only witness to what had happened with Luba, she remembered. Luba was Keeper of the Aurameres, but she was also Cornelia's worst enemy. Luba thought the new Guardians were totally incompetent. But ironically, Luba was the one who messed up, big-time. The Aurameres had collided to create an all-powerful Altermere. When the Altermere and Cornelia came face-to-face, Cornelia had absorbed the Altermere and became all-powerful.

Luba then came to Cornelia's apartment. The Oracle had ordered her to try to undo her mistake. But Luba's plan was to stop Cornelia and to prove her inadequacy as a Guardian. Napoleon had been suspicious of her right away, but Cornelia hadn't had the good sense to listen to him.

Luba couldn't stop me in the end, though, Cornelia thought. My power was ultimately stronger than hers, and I managed to revive Caleb. That really got Luba mad! She tried to punish me – along with all my friends. If Caleb hadn't stepped in, who knows where we'd be right now?

Cornelia opened the door to her room to say hi to Napoleon and was surprised to hear him hiss. "Calm down there, tiger!" Cornelia said. "It's only me." She tried to pet him, but the cat just arched his back and bared his teeth. Something strange was going on. Cornelia was pretty sure she knew who the culprit was.

"What did you do to him, Lilian?" she asked, turning to look at her sister, who was cowering in the doorway. "Did you try to put make-up on him again?"

"He loves it when I do that," Lilian protested. "But this time it's not my fault! He's been like that ever since Mummy's friend got here."

That's interesting, Cornelia thought.

Napoleon has good judgment. What bad thing does he see in Sandra Doubman, beyond her disastrous fashion sense?

Guess I need to take a better look at her, Cornelia thought. She headed back downstairs, just in time to overhear some bad news.

"And I made a reservation at that absolutely marvellous spa near Riddlescott!" Sandra squealed to Cornelia's dad. "Elizabeth told me you were going to the area, so I thought . . ."

So she's not just here for a visit, Cornelia realised. We're stuck with her. I thought I didn't want to be alone. But this lady is almost as scary as Nerissa! Having her for company isn't what I would call a relaxing vacation.

FOUR

As her mum's car sped through Heatherfield, Will rolled down her window and took a big breath of the fresh air. The air of my hometown, Will thought.

It had taken her a while to feel she belonged there, but something about returning from her trip made Will realise how much she'd settled in. She felt peaceful and satisfied, for once.

I guess that's what a vacation's supposed to do! she thought with a smile.

The whole Nerissa-nightmare thing was pretty creepy, but everything else was good – she was getting along with her friends and her mum, and the best thing of all was still waiting for her: her reunion with Matt. It was getting closer every minute!

Will was trying to figure out when she'd get in touch with him. He knows when mum and I are coming back from our vacation, she remembered. So, do I call him right away? Or will that look too desperate? I could leave it till the next day. Or even the day after. But then what if he thinks I don't want to see him?

It had only been a few minutes since they'd said goodbye, but Will was already missing Cornelia. Her friend would have known exactly what to do.

Will's mum turned in to their street and pulled into a parking spot right outside their building. She was about to open her door when Will noticed a man waving to them from the curb.

Oh, no, Will thought. Not now. She slumped down in her seat a little. "What is he doing here?" she asked her mum quietly.

He was her history teacher, Mr. Collins. Seeing him outside of school was bad enough. But it got worse: Mr. Collins was also her mum's boyfriend.

"Relax, Will!" Mrs. Vandom said lightly, ignoring Will's pouting. "Dean has other plans for his vacation."

"Thank goodness," Will said, sighing. "I'm sorry, Mum. It's just no fun to have to put up with your teacher all summer long!" She deliberately avoided her mother's look (which she knew probably wasn't happy) as she climbed out of the car.

I won't start a fight, Will said to herself, over and over again. I won't start a fight. Things are going too well. But why does he have to be here now? she asked her mum silently. You're the one who wants to be all close again. Do you think this helps?

Mr. Collins, oblivious to Will's inner musings, bounded over to the car like an eager puppy. "Hi, Susan!" he cried. "Hi, Will! Am I in time to convince you not to go?"

"No harm in trying!" said Will's mum, smiling.

Overdoing the chivalry, Mr. Collins insisted on taking Will's bags inside. Will could totally imagine what was going through her mum's mind: *Such a gentleman!* Whatever, Will thought. The only upside was that she got a moment to look him over without being noticed. Blue-plaid pants and a loose white shirt. He wouldn't dare wear that outfit to school, she thought. It looks just like pyjamas!

"A nice cultural trip would do you guys some good," Mr. Collins said as he followed Will's mum upstairs and into the apartment. He still sounded just like a teacher.

Will's mum tossed her bouncy, black hair. "Sorry! Maybe next summer!" she replied with a smile.

Let the flirting begin, thought Will. She stuck her tongue out at Mr. Collins when she was sure he wasn't looking. *That's for barging in where you're not wanted,* she told him silently. *And getting between me and my mum. Again.*

"Come on! Come with me!" Mr. Collins begged. "We'll see the most beautiful art the city has to offer!"

"Waiting in line outside a museum in the boiling sun? That's not my idea of a vacation." Will's mum retorted.

"Bah!" her boyfriend said.

"*My* idea of vacation is called Club Tropical. Everything included. Picturesque forests! Beaches! Swimming pools! Concert halls! Shops! Saunas!" Will's mum went on and on.

"Sounds like one of those places where you spend all your time trying to avoid the organisers," said Mr. Collins. Will smiled in spite of herself. He had a point. She wasn't a big fan of places like that, either. "They don't give you time to breathe! You have to have fun, even if you don't want to!" he added with a sigh.

Will's mum was still daydreaming. "Whirlpools! Archery! Windsurfing! All-you-can-eat breakfasts! Theme dinners!"

This has got to stop, Will thought as she collapsed onto the red couch in her living room. Her mum was so weird, but at least it gave her an idea of what *not* to say to Matt.

"And when it's all over, the vacationers can't wait to get back to work!" Mr. Collins continued, trying to get Will's mum's attention.

It was as if Mrs. Vandom hadn't heard him. "Candlelight dinners! Dashing swim instructors!" she chanted.

Mr. Collins did a double take. "Dashing who?" he asked, looking pained. Will almost felt sorry for him . . . for a minute.

Will's mum waved her hand in the air dismissively. "It was the only way to get you to stop talking," she joked.

Driiing! the doorbell rang. "That must be the

skirt they're delivering from the dry cleaner," Will's mum called out. "Would you get the door, Will?" she asked.

Her daughter was already off the couch and halfway toward the door. "Sure," she muttered, rolling her eyes. "My pleasure. Good thing I didn't stay at Irma's for another day. I would have missed all the excitement!" Actually, Will wouldn't have minded going to the dry cleaner in person – anything to get away from the love-birds. But going to the door was better than nothing.

Will slid the lock back and swung the door open. The deliveryman stood there in a shiny red motorcycle helmet and tinted visor, with only one thin, clear strip around the eyes allowing him to see.

"Hello, Will!" the guy said, surprising her. How did the delivery guy know her name?

She had no clue who it was. She couldn't even really see the guy's eyes! Whom did she know who had got a job doing deliveries this summer? Will wondered. Think. *Think*, she urged herself. But her mind was a blank.

"Will?" the guy repeated. "Don't you recog-nise me?"

"Sure! Um . . . I know I've seen that helmet somewhere before. . . ." Will stammered.

Why do you always have to sound so dumb? she chastised herself immediately.

At least the guy wasn't going to make her guess any longer. "Oh, all right," he said. "Is this better?" He lifted the helmet and smiled.

Will grabbed the side of the door in shock. It wasn't a deliveryman. It wasn't someone she'd forgotten. It wasn't someone who belonged at her apartment. Or in Heatherfield. Or on the earth, for that matter.

It was Caleb, looking hotter than ever. Cornelia's Caleb . . . at her door!

Will had read about people being made speechless. Sometimes she'd wished it would happen to her, since she never knew what was going to fly out of her mouth. But she hadn't really believed it could happen – until now.

What is he doing here? Will wondered. And why does he have to look so *completely* cool on his first trip to Heatherfield? The motorcycle jacket Caleb was wearing set off the deep blue of his eyes to perfection, and his chin-length hair followed the contours of his sculpted cheekbones. Will didn't dare look down at her grungy jeans and tank top. She was just glad it was Cornelia's boyfriend, and not her own, catching her so totally off guard . . . and messy!

Caleb didn't seem to have time to wait for Will to find her voice. He lowered his head and said in a hushed tone, "I'm here to ask for your help, Will. Cornelia's in danger!"

What? Will thought, instantly in crisis mode. Where can we go to talk? The doorway to her apartment wasn't exactly private, but there'd be her mum and Mr. Collins to deal with if they went inside.

Maybe that's not so bad, Will decided. They're so wrapped up in each other that they probably won't even notice Caleb! It could work . . . maybe.

"Um . . . come on in," she stumbled awkwardly. "We can talk it over. But you've got to be wrong. I just saw Cornelia outside her house and . . ."

Following Will into the living room, Caleb didn't let her finish. "I know. She's leaving right this minute for Riddlescott Lake!" He perched nervously on the edge of the couch and added, "Unfortunately, there's a woman going along with her family. She says she's an old friend of

Cornelia's mum's, but she's not. That woman is Luba, the Keeper of the Aurameres!"

Will was dumbfounded. It couldn't be, she thought. It shouldn't be. Beings from Candracar didn't usually pop up in Heatherfield unannounced. Luba was the last one the Guardians needed to see – the cat-woman had been nothing but trouble for them. "What?" she asked. "How did . . ."

Caleb scowled and made a fist. He was definitely frustrated. "She got away, Will! I was supposed to capture her, but she got away from me." He bent over and hid his face in his hands.

Ok, thought Will, taking a deep breath. *This is not good. Luba wasn't supposed to leave Candracar – she escaped. And Caleb's the Herald of Candracar now, which means he carries messages between the worlds and handles stuff on all the worlds for the Oracle. So he's the one who's supposed to bring her back.*

But something was not making any sense to Will. Luba had seen Cornelia restoring Caleb to his boy form. She knew how strong the feelings were between the two of them. She knew the power of their love . . . and the damage it could inflict. Why would Luba ever seek Cornelia out? Will asked herself. Luba knows Caleb won't be able to resist finding her. Isn't Luba taking a major chance that she'll be discovered?

"The Oracle was wrong to entrust me with this task!" Caleb moaned. "This is all my fault!"

He looked so sad.

Kind of like Cornelia did when Caleb was a flower, Will remembered.

She hadn't known what to do then, and she didn't know what to do now. It felt weird enough to be alone with Caleb. Will didn't know him that well, except through Cornelia. And now he was asking for her help.

Suddenly, Will's leader skills kicked in. "That's not true!" she cried. "It's *not* your fault. Here's the deal." The words flew out of Will's mouth as she put it all together. "Luba, of all people, knows everything about you and Cornelia. And she must also know that you're chasing her. What if she's using Cornelia as a sort of insurance policy? Maybe she's thinking nothing can happen to her if she sticks to your girlfriend like glue. Maybe she has other plans for being here besides capturing Cornelia."

Caleb thought it over. "You might be right,"

he said. "And she definitely knows I'm following her. Somehow the Keeper can sense my presence whenever I'm nearby."

He jumped off the sofa and put his hands on Will's shoulders. "Maybe *you* could get close to Cornelia without making Luba suspicious," Caleb begged.

She started to say something like "I'm not so sure I'd manage. . . ." But the look in Caleb's eyes was enough to persuade anybody, and she stopped. Will knew she could never leave her friend in Luba's clutches – much less leave Caleb high and dry.

The only problem is my mum, Will realised. We're leaving tomorrow morning. I can't tell her I have to run an errand in Riddlescott Lake now!

Just then, Will heard her mum's voice calling from the bedroom. "Will, was that my skirt? Can you bring it in here, please?" she asked.

There wasn't a second to lose. Will squeezed her eyes shut and balled her hands up in fists. One by one, she banished all of her thoughts and worries from her mind. Luba? Gone. Her mum? Gone. Cornelia and Caleb? Gone. Will breathed deeply and concentrated on the one thing that mattered now: an astral drop. A perfect double who could stay there while Will went off with Caleb to find Cornelia and keep her safe from Luba. She'd made mistakes with astral drops in the past. But this time it *has* to work, Will told herself. This time I will do it right.

Even with her eyes closed, Will could tell that the light was changing around her. She was glowing! A stream of clear blue light swirled around her body as Will envisioned another Will, the Will who would take her place.

Abruptly the glow disappeared, and Will opened her eyes. Her astral drop stood next to her, looking a little confused.

Do I really look like that? Will couldn't help wondering. So rumpled? So nervous?

Seeing her astral drop was as weird as hearing her voice on tape . . . but Will couldn't dwell on that now. She filled her astral drop in on the basics: she was about to leave for vacation with her mum, and she had just spent a great week with her friends. And, oh, yeah, she and her mum were getting along . . . for now. That was just about all she needed to know.

Will was dying to change into clean clothes, but she couldn't risk being in the apartment that long – she didn't want to be spotted with Astral Will. Quickly rummaging around in the hall closet for a jacket, she crept out with Caleb and walked as quietly as she could.

She followed Caleb down the stairs, her heart pounding. What does Luba have in store for us this time? she wondered. Will felt a little scared of the unknown.

But Caleb must be even more scared than I am, she realised. Cornelia would want me to put him at his ease.

She grabbed the extra helmet from Caleb's bike and took a deep breath.

"So, my perfect double will enjoy the perfect resort vacation," she announced, following Caleb as he walked quickly down the street with his motorcycle. "In any case, this time I made a good astral drop! I normally make a big mess of things!"

Will instantly wished she hadn't said that. It wasn't going to make Caleb feel better if she admitted to making mistakes all the time! All she could hope now was that this time things would be better. They had to save Cornelia!

FIVE

Mr. Collins rubbed his chin and squinted a little harder at his trusty pocket atlas. "So," he told Susan Vandom, "by taking a shortcut through Shatterford, I could stop by to visit you at the resort!" He was determined to find a way to make it work. He wanted to spend more time with her.

Susan was totally distracted. "The more I have to do, the less Will helps me!" she complained. "Would you hand me those shoes?" A suitcase was open on her bed, and she was frantically packing it for her trip.

It could be *our* trip for a while, Mr. Collins reminded himself. If only I can persuade her.

It always made Mr. Collins laugh to think about how the kids at school counted the days till summer vacation.

How do they think the teachers feel? he thought with a smile. The vacation is the best perk of the job! But Susan doesn't get the same amount of time off, so every moment of her vacation is precious. I can't let the whole week fly by without some time for *us* in it, he thought.

Mr. Collins was ready to give up a day of roaming through museums if he had to. Visiting the resort wouldn't be *so* bad.

Neither of us wants to give up our independence, and I can respect that, he thought. Still, we need some downtime in this relationship. Without the pressures of Susan's job. Without my school life getting in the way. If roasting on the beach is the answer . . . I'm in.

Not so long ago, Mr. Collins wouldn't even have considered going away with Susan. Travelling with Susan meant travelling with Will, too, and that would have been a bad idea. Will didn't like the idea of her mum dating her teacher. And Mr. Collins didn't always like the idea of dating his student's parent, either. He looked forward to the day when he could laugh with Will about how awkward it had been for *him*. It was hard not to give her special treatment at school, but all in all he thought he'd done a good job of keeping things professional.

Things seemed better now, though. His feelings for Will had grown and deepened along with his feelings for her mother. Mr. Collins and Will weren't exactly friends, but they'd come to accept each other.

Hey, I'd say she looked pretty happy to see me today, Mr. Collins said to himself. He'd learned that there were two cardinal rules for getting along with Susan's daughter. One was that they not talk about school at home or about home at school. The other was that he never get in the middle of arguments between mother and daughter. He made it a point to steer clear of family conflicts.

Susan was staring in his direction, her hands on her hips. What? wondered Mr. Collins. Oh, the shoes. He'd forgotten all about them. Where is my mind today? he wondered. I guess I really do need to get away!

He grabbed the shoes, handed them over, and tried again. "We could spend at least one day together!" he said. Susan put the shoes next to a row of socks she'd already packed. "Are you even listening?" he asked.

The *breep! breep!* of the phone interrupted him.

"Of course I am, Dean!" Susan replied absently. "Would you mind getting that phone for me?"

Mr. Collins started toward the phone, but then his eyes landed on the atlas, lying open to the page he'd been looking at, and suddenly he saw another possible route. Oh, no, he thought, I had it all wrong.

On second thought, by taking the shortcut through Shatterford, I'd actually be going farther. I could go into Higgletown and . . .

He remembered to grab the phone just before the answering machine did. "Hello?" he said, a little breathlessly.

A boy's voice on the other end of the line said, "Hello? Um . . . May I speak to Will?"

"Who's calling, please?" Mr. Collins asked.

The boy's name was Matt. Mentally, Mr. Collins scanned through all the Matts he knew at school. There was the Matt who was always in detention and the Matt who played soccer. And then there was the cool Matt, the Matt who was the lead singer in some band.

Now that I think about it, this kid kind of sounds like him, Mr. Collins realised. He's not in Will's crowd, though. Is she friends with him? Or, is she *more* than friends? Very interesting. You can look at a kid in class all year and never get a real sense of who he is or who his friends are.

"Hold on a second, Matt. I'll go get her," said Mr. Collins. He walked into the living room carrying the phone, but Will wasn't there. She wasn't in the kitchen, either. He was about to knock on her bedroom door when he happened to see a flash of light on the wall, a reflection from something outside. He walked to the window, and there she was. On the sidewalk below, Will was adjusting a helmet and getting ready to climb onto a motorcycle behind a boy.

Strange, he thought. I didn't know Will rode motorcycles. She must not like this Matt, Mr. Collins realised. Not if she's leaving with that guy down there.

Mr. Collins spoke into the receiver again and explained it to Matt. "Ah, there she is. Outside. Sorry, but she's just gone out."

"Do you know where she's going?" Matt

asked. "Any idea when she'll be back?"

Mr. Collins still didn't know much about Will. He had no clue as to what she did with her friends or where they went. He didn't even know when her curfew was! I can only tell this guy what I see, Mr. Collins thought. So he did. "She's getting on a motorcycle with some kid, but I don't know who he is."

Matt's voice sounded strained. "A guy?" he asked.

"A guy," Mr. Collins confirmed.

"Are you sure?" Matt insisted. He did not sound happy.

Oh, dear, thought Mr. Collins. I hope I haven't said the wrong thing. "I'm positive," he said.

Before he could say goodbye, the phone went dead. Matt had hung up on him! Mr. Collins stared at the phone and shook his head. When will kids learn to be polite?

The light from the window was full and bright, and it illuminated the pocket atlas. Mr. Collins picked it up once more and muttered, "Hmmm. Where was I, again? Shatterford! Higgletown and . . ." He traced the route with his finger when a thought suddenly occurred to him: Will's not supposed to be going anywhere! She's going on vacation . . . with Susan!

The teachers at school were always trading horror stories about good kids who sneaked out of their houses and got into major trouble. Mr. Collins had never pegged Will for that type, but teenagers were totally unpredictable.

I just wish I didn't have to be the one to break it to Susan, thought Mr. Collins.

Telling her would not go over well. *And* it would break his all-important rule – he'd be getting in the middle of what was sure to be a major blowup. He'd be starting it, in fact!

Susan's going to go ballistic, Mr. Collins groaned to himself. And Will will think I tattled on her.

He walked slowly back into Susan's room.

Sure enough, Susan's eyes bugged out when he told her.

"Will? On a motorcycle? With a stranger?" she asked, her voice growing louder with each question. She ran to the downstairs window to see if she could spot Will, but the motorcycle was long gone.

"Dean, I can't believe this! Why didn't you stop her?" Susan asked accusingly.

Mr. Collins hung his head like one of his seventh graders and said, "I . . . I was distracted! I was studying the road map and . . ."

Just then, the TV in the family room went on, and a familiar face poked out from around the side of the couch. "Could you two keep it down?" Will asked. "I can't hear the TV!"

Susan glared at Mr. Collins as if to say, "What were you thinking, giving me a heart attack like that?" He could feel himself blushing for the first time in who knew how long. But I saw her! he thought. She was right there!

"By the way," Will said in a bored tone, "no skirt from the dry cleaner's. It was just some guy selling encyclopedias."

When Mr. Collins dared to make eye contact with Susan, she snapped. "I am seriously thinking of asking you not to take that shortcut through Shatterford!"

He tried to defend himself. "So I was wrong. The important thing is that Will is home, safe and sound." To himself he added: And I am slowly starting to lose my mind. I *really* do need a vacation, even if I have to go alone!

SIX

Caleb pushed his motorcycle down the street and wondered how long it would take for Will to realise there was something wrong with his bike. After all, he was walking next to it – not riding. She kept talking about her problems making astral drops. But she'd just made one, Caleb thought. What was she so worried about? He was pretty impressed by the way the redhead had come up with a plan and carried it out, all within a matter of seconds. Caleb didn't usually see the Guardians' work up close. Was it always that efficient? Caleb wondered. He wished he could say the same for his own magic. But so far he didn't have much to show for his time in Heatherfield.

"Normally, I make a real mess of things," Will was saying. Caleb brought his attention back to his companion.

That's exactly how I feel, Caleb realised. It's like she's reading my mind. Can she do that?

He wouldn't have put it past her. Will was a far more accomplished Guardian than he'd realised.

"I have problems handling my powers, too," Caleb admitted.

Will looked at him skeptically. "You? Mr. Perfection?" she laughed lightheartedly.

"Very funny," said Caleb.

She doesn't believe me, he thought. She only knows the person I was in Meridian. There I was the hero. Now I'm just like any other guy – only more awkward!

Caleb knew he was going to have to be straight with her, even if he found it humiliating. "Take this motorcycle, for instance. I should be riding it, not pushing it."

"Come on! Anybody can run out of gas!" Will said with a shrug.

"Gas has nothing to do with it. Really, I don't think I'll be able to take you to Riddlescott Lake." Caleb emphasised each word so that Will would understand.

He watched as she took a moment to figure out the situation. When she did, her eyes practically popped out of her head. Caleb felt his face turn red. With all the magic in the world, he still couldn't figure out how to ride a motorcycle.

"But . . . but . . . you're the Herald of Candracar," Will said in bewilderment. "And thanks to Cornelia, you even have a copy of our five powers inside of you! When she gave them to you and turned you back into a human – didn't that make you stronger?"

"I know, but they can't help me," said Caleb. "Learning to ride takes more than just a snap of your fingers. Plus, I've never had any practice!" He hoped his voice sounded lighthearted. Inside, he was feeling anything but.

"It doesn't make any sense!" Will cried. "How did you get all the way to my house?"

"I walked! And I was going so slow I risked getting a ticket for loitering!" said Caleb ruefully. "I come from Meridian, and, believe me, over there it's a lot easier to get around!"

"Well, then, I guess it's true that nobody's perfect," Will replied, throwing up her hands.

Caleb rolled his eyes. I really wish Will would stop saying that, he thought. I mean, I guess I can see how I seemed perfect in Meridian. Cornelia and her friends came along just as things were starting to go my way. But they gave me too much credit for being brave. In reality, there's no way I could have toppled Prince Phobos without them!

He was worried about Cornelia now. Everything in this place was new to him. Caleb knew Meridian, where everything was dark, and Candracar, where all was bright white, and neither had prepared him for the dazzling variety of colour here in Heatherfield. It was exciting to see where Cornelia came from, but it was a little overwhelming to take it in without her by his side. He had a million questions and no guide.

Why does everything move so fast? Why does it seem so loud?

And then there were his powers. Possessing a copy of the Guardians' powers might have made him feel invincible in this new place . . . if only he had known how to use them. Cornelia and her friends had total (well, almost total) mastery over earth, air, fire, water, energy – not to mention the Heart. But to Caleb those powers felt as uncomfortable as his motorcycle jacket, which made an irritating swishing sound every time he moved his arms. He never knew when the magic would work, which was making him uneasy.

As he pushed the motorcycle toward a huge, domed building, he saw there were people lined up beside it and strange noises coming from inside its open doors. A huge vehicle groaned to a stop in front of it, and more people began to climb off, clutching large bags.

"Luckily for us, there's public transportation!" Will announced cheerfully.

"Right!" said Caleb. "You use buses here!" For that was what they were. The buses seemed slow and smelly, a last resort if you couldn't travel in a car. Would this even work? Caleb wondered. How long would it take? What if they didn't get to Cornelia in time? He didn't like leaving *everything* up to Will, but he didn't really have a choice.

He tried to make light of the situation. "Don't worry, Cornelia," he said, making his voice extremely deep. "I'm coming to save you! I just have to stamp my ticket!" Returning to his usual voice, he added, "Can you imagine?"

"Oh, stop," Will said, laughing. "By travelling like this, we won't be so conspicuous."

Will found their bus as easily as she'd made the astral drop, and, before they boarded it, Caleb turned to her for some instructions. "Should I get rid of this motorcycle?" he asked. "And everything else?" Caleb couldn't wait to take off his gloves and his helmet. He was ready to leave it all there at the station.

But Will didn't feel the same way. "No, um, I want to keep my helmet on for a little while longer," she said softly, her cheeks growing slightly pink. "You never know. . . . My mum thinks I'm at home, and, well, somebody could see us together!"

She had something on her mind, Caleb thought. Or . . . some*one*. A boy, maybe?

Caleb could see how it might be a problem if another boy spotted them together. In Candracar, he often worried that someone would come along and get a crush on Cornelia. He totally understood about jealousy.

He still didn't know Will very well – in Meridian he'd devoted most of his attention to Cornelia or to fighting Phobos's forces.

Suddenly, though, Caleb felt a real connection. If we're both in love, then we're on an equal footing, he realised. Somehow it made him feel much better about having to rely on her.

Both of us are vulnerable, he thought.

With a smile on his face, he followed Will on to the bus. As she settled into her seat in the back of the bus, Will finally removed her helmet. Caleb sat down next to her. The seat was caved in and uncomfortable, and the bus shuddered with every turn of the narrow, twisting road between Heatherfield and Riddlescott Lake. Will closed her eyes, but Caleb was fascinated by the scenery. He'd never seen mountains or woods like those before, and he couldn't stop thinking about how Cornelia had travelled along this same road just a short time ago. He couldn't wait to hold her in his arms. Until they were together, his heart would ache with the fear that Luba would hurt her. Once he was with her, though, Caleb knew she'd be safe. Nothing would get between them; their love was that strong. He just had to trust in the fact that Will would get him where he needed to go. He just had to find a way to relax.

The motion of the bus had almost lulled Caleb to sleep when a small head popped up from around the seat in front of him. A boy with raggedy blond hair and a face full of freckles pointed to Caleb's cheek. "Is that a tattoo on your face, or are you just turning green?" the child asked him.

Caleb instinctively put his hands to the green spots on his cheeks. They were the only evidence still remaining that he'd once been a flower, and he knew that they looked strange there on earth. He fumbled, looking for the right answer.

Once again Will came to his rescue. "Um, little boy? I think your mother is calling you, down there in the front of the bus!" She pointed in the opposite direction from their seats.

The boy didn't budge. "No, she's not!" he whined. "And the driver sent me back here. I'm not supposed to talk to him while he's driving!"

Will glanced in a sidelong way at Caleb and grumbled, "Well, I'm out of ideas."

The kid was staring rudely at Caleb. "I think you've got a funny face! Are you from another country?" he demanded to know. Caleb felt Will cringe beside him.

"Better than that!" Caleb said boldly. "I come from another world!"

Will's jaw dropped open. "Caleb!" she warned in a whisper. His mission was supposed to be a secret.

"You want to get rid of this brat, don't you?" Caleb whispered back. "Trust me!" *Like I trust you,* he urged silently. *We're in this together.*

"Another world? Yeah, right," the kid sneered. "So what's she?" he asked, jabbing his thumb in Will's direction. "Like, an alien or something?"

"Oh, no," Caleb explained patiently. "She's a fairy, and she's going to Riddlescott Lake to save her friend Cornelia." Caleb put his fingers in the air and scratched the air with them as if they were the claws of some terrible creature. "An evil witch named Luba has tricked her with a spell!" Even as he said the words, Caleb knew the little boy would never believe it.

But, he added silently, *maybe I can make him go away.*

"Your story is so pathetic," said the kid, shaking his head.

Caleb ignored the comment and continued. "I'm a wizard! It's my job to capture the witch and take her back to a place called Candracar!" He did his best to avoid Will's worried look.

"If you were really magical," the kid pointed out, "you wouldn't be riding on this thing!"

Nodding his head sagely, Caleb agreed. "That's so true," he said. "We would have transported ourselves, right? But my powers are brand new. "I don't know how to control them yet."

The kid put his hands on his hips and looked skeptically at Caleb. "My generation isn't as gullible as you think. I'm not buying it!"

"Oh, really? Well, watch this!" Caleb said. He lifted his hands and touched the tip of one index finger to the tip of the other. "If I wanted to transport you, all I'd have to do is put my fingers together like this, then point to the place where I wanted to send you!"

The kid was picking on him, but Caleb was having fun teasing him right back. For just a moment, he forgot about Cornelia and Luba. He forgot about the place and the predicament he was in. He relaxed in a way he hadn't managed since he'd arrived on earth.

Caleb's moment of peace was also a moment of magic. He hadn't managed to transport much since he'd left Candracar, but suddenly an electric crackle flashed around the boy. Then, with a sharp *shaaa*, the boy disappeared! He had been transported away . . . hopefully safely.

Caleb's eyes met Will's. He wasn't sure what he saw there. Fear? Anger? Pride? Before he could figure it out, he heard a sizzling *aaartz!* at the front of the bus, and the boy reappeared – beside the driver!

"Aaagh!" shouted the driver, startled.

"Aaagh!" screamed the boy in terror.

The bus swerved around a hairpin turn in the road, but nothing could disturb Caleb's sense of calm.

I did it, he thought, when I let my worries go. The magic is at my disposal, ready to help Cornelia. I just have to banish my fears, as I did back in Meridian. I have to open my mind and go with the flow!

SEVEN

Even way in the back of the bus, it was impossible for Will to ignore what was going on in the front of the bus. She glanced at Caleb and shook her head, as if to say, "I can't believe you did that!"

"Hey, kid!" the driver yelled at the freckle-faced boy. "I told you to go sit in the back!"

The boy clutched the driver's arm and glanced fearfully at Will and Caleb. "N – no!" he stuttered. "I'm not going back down there!" The driver ignored the pleas for mercy and pushed him down the aisle.

The boy scooted halfway to the back, keeping his head down so he wouldn't make eye contact with either Will or Caleb.

"Mummy! Mummy!" he cried. "I'm telling you, they are a wizard and a fairy! They told me so!" He pointed at Will and Caleb with a trembling finger.

"That's enough, Boyd," his mother said firmly. It was obvious she was used to Boyd's behaviour. Sighing, she pointed to the seat beside her. "It's time to sit down and stop bothering people."

Huffing, the kid climbed over his mother's lap and flopped into his seat. Then he crossed his arms and stared angrily out the window.

As Will watched she couldn't help thinking that Boyd had got what was coming to him. He had really been annoying Caleb! But Will could also easily imagine how it felt to be that boy just then. After all, it wasn't very long ago that she had felt like a scared little kid. She'd been totally freaked out the first time she saw magic, too.

And what would happen if I tried to tell my mum some of the things I've seen in Meridian and Candracar? Will wondered. She wouldn't believe me any more than Boyd's mum believes him. She would think I was losing my mind!

Will sighed and sank deeper into her seat.

Sometimes she wished she could just come out and tell her mum about her powers. It would make things so much easier between them if she could just tell the truth. But sometimes honesty wasn't the most feasible, practical policy, Will reminded herself. Mum wouldn't want to know the dangers Will had been in. She wouldn't want to know about the enemies Will had made or the things she had done. Total honesty was more than she could handle. She would completely flip out!

I mean, what would Mum say if she saw what Caleb had just done? Will thought.

Will tried to decide which of her favourite expressions her mum would have used if she had become aware of Caleb and his powers.

He really had taken a risk with that little boy. Will leaned over to him. "I can't believe you transported that boy!" she said softly.

"Don't worry," Caleb said, sounding like the old, brave Caleb Will knew. "Everyone else was sleeping. Nobody saw a thing!"

Will wasn't worried, really. At first she hadn't liked the way Caleb was spilling their secrets to Boyd, but it had been obvious the kid wasn't going to believe what Caleb told him. Now she was just excited about the way Caleb had transported the boy with a flick of his fingers!

"If you can do that," she asked Caleb, "why didn't we just use magic to go to Riddlescott Lake?"

Caleb looked at the floor. "I don't know your world, Will," he said. "The things! The places! Everything is so strange to me." A shadow crossed his face, and Will wasn't sure if it came from outside the bus or from inside him.

He's not like he used to be, she realised. He seems so much sadder.

"If I tried to cover a great distance," Caleb continued, "I'd risk getting lost! I could end up right in Luba's hands."

I can understand that, thought Will. I know what it's like to be scared of messing up with magic! It's strange, though, to see Caleb so different from the way he was in Meridian. He was so powerful and courageous when he was leading the rebels. But that's when he was in the place he knew the best. He's lost some of his confidence here on earth.

Maybe *I* could transport us, Will thought. Things seem to be going my way – after all, that astral drop I made was perfect!

She'd missed being able to use her magic when the Guardians were fighting. Now she was eager to get back into the swing of things. "You think I could transport people and objects, too?" Will asked Caleb.

"I've only been able to do it since I got a copy of your five powers," Caleb explained. "So, I guess, theoretically, you could."

Will lifted her fingers in the air as Caleb had done, but paused. She didn't want to try it just then. Maybe some other time, she decided.

Not that I'm scared or anything, she added defensively. But we're almost at Riddlescott Lake. And then we'll get reinforcements. There's no point in risking any more attention on this trip.

Thinking of the reinforcements – her friends – made Will smile. "I really hope Irma, Taranee, and Hay Lin are on their way," she said to Caleb.

Caleb nodded. "They'll catch up," he said reassuringly. "It's lucky you managed to contact them!"

"Thanks to my trusty cell phone," Will beamed. What had people done without them?

Her cell phone seemed to like the praise.

Better look at my display! the phone said cheerfully. *There's an unanswered phone call!*

Will shot a quick look at Caleb, but he didn't seem bothered by the talking cell phone.

He must not know that cell phones don't talk! she laughed to herself. To him, any phone is probably unusual!

Will had been able to talk to electronic devices since the moment she had acquired her power along with the Heart of Candracar. She couldn't quite explain it, but it came in handy. Will kept up a running dialogue with her computer and even her refrigerator. Her cell phone, though, was the chattiest of all.

"Oh, no!" she told the phone, keeping her voice low, so that nobody on the bus would overhear. "Don't tell me it was Matt!"

I'm a cell phone, not a mind reader, the phone shot back. *Whoever it was called from a pay phone.*

There was no voice mail, though, and no text message either. It wasn't like Matt not to leave one, if it even was Matt, Will told herself. And now she'd never know.

"I'm so dumb!" she said to Caleb. "Now I'll spend all my time hoping he calls back!" Then she gasped. She hadn't meant to admit she was waiting for a call from a boy. Caleb didn't even know Matt!

Caleb's next words eased her mind. He sighed. "I know what you mean. It's not easy to be separated from people who are special to you." Will thought she detected tears glinting in his eyes, but he turned away from her abruptly and looked at the scenery again.

Will wondered what he was thinking.

Well, duh. He's thinking about Cornelia, she told herself. But what, exactly? Is he remembering a time they spent together? Is he dreaming of being with her again?

Will let her imagination run a little wild. Was Matt thinking about her that way at that very moment? Was he reviewing their date in his mind over and over, as she was? Was he dying to hold her hand?

Will shook herself back to reality.

Things with Matt aren't even close to what Cornelia and Caleb have, she thought. I should just face it. Matt and I hardly know each other, while Cornelia and Caleb are meant to be.

It made Will feel lonely all over again.

But she was in an optimistic frame of mind.

There was another way to see it, she decided. She didn't have what she wanted right then – and neither did Caleb. Both of them were suffering from being apart. And they could be there for each other as they waited for things to change! Will had been feeling closer to Caleb all day, but this thought cemented their bond in her mind.

Will wished she had the words to comfort Caleb, to make him see that she shared a portion of his sorrow. She could see his reflection in the window, staring into space.

And then, out of nowhere, he said, "At times, what destiny unites, life divides."

His words sent a chill down Will's spine. That's exactly what I was thinking, she thought. We are *so* on the same wavelength! I couldn't have said it better myself.

EIGHT

Cornelia lagged behind her family as Mr. Krinkle, the owner of the house they were renting at Riddlescott Lake, unlocked the door.

She had to admit, the place was gorgeous. It was perched on the edge of the lake, with a sweeping front porch and even a private pier . . . in the middle of nowhere. There wasn't another house or another person in sight. Cornelia's dad always liked to pick an isolated spot for the family vacation – "As different as possible from the city," he would say.

This house sure fits the bill, Cornelia thought.

Her family followed Mr. Krinkle inside, but Cornelia lingered on the doorstep for a moment and sighed.

Well, at least it's not a complete dump, she thought. It's a great place to spend a week. But it would be a thousand times better if my friends were here, too. And a million times better if Sandra Doubman stayed home!

Cornelia had had about as much of Sandra Doubman as she could stand. Her mother's friend had insisted on sitting in the backseat, wedged between Cornelia and her sister, for the entire ride to Riddlescott Lake.

How often did she have to grab my arm to get my attention? Cornelia asked herself. I wouldn't be surprised if I had a bruise!

Sandra was full of stories about when she and Mrs. Hale were younger. But Mum's told me all those stories before, Cornelia thought, and when Sandra tells them, they never seem to end!

It was bad enough that Sandra had intruded on the trip to the lake – now she was going to intrude for the whole week.

Her reservations at the spa supposedly fell through, Cornelia glowered. That's why she needs to stay with us. Right! I doubt it's even true. I bet she planned this all along!

She took a deep breath and finally went inside, where she was relieved to find that

Sandra and her mum had gone upstairs. Sandra was probably picking out her room. The biggest one, Cornelia figured. It felt a little stuffy, and Cornelia wondered when this place had last been rented. She walked around the first floor opening windows while her dad talked to Mr. Krinkle.

"As you can see, the house has a stunning view, to say the least," its owner said.

Mr. Hale nodded politely. "Just like in the brochure I received, Mr. Krinkle." Cornelia could tell her dad was ready for him to leave.

But Mr. Krinkle didn't take the hint. "Ah, yes!" he exclaimed. "A real paradise! Even if it's my duty to warn you . . ." He raised a cautionary finger and lowered his voice dramatically. "Riddlescott Lake is believed to be a bit of a Loch Ness!"

One glance at her sister's face and Cornelia knew there was going to be trouble. Lilian looked enraptured.

Puh-leeze, Cornelia thought. Tell me she doesn't believe this.

"I don't like to frighten my tenants," Mr. Krinkle continued, "but a couple of sightings have been reported in this very spot."

Lilian's eyes grew wide. "There's a monster in the lake? A real monster?" she asked. She covered her mouth in fear.

Cornelia's nerves were already raw from Sandra Doubman's grating voice and overwhelming perfume. Another time, she might have laughed off her sister's fears, but not now. *If only she knew what I've seen in Meridian,* she thought. *Forget about lake monsters. How about slimy blue slugs? How about Prince Phobos, the embodiment of all evil? I'll show you scary! And those things were* real*! How can Lilian believe this silly story?*

Cornelia's dad didn't seem impressed, either. He squinted at the brochure in his hand and said, "Krinkle! Here it says you're also the . . ."

". . . Mayor of the nearby town of Riddlescott," Mr. Krinkle interrupted with a silly little bow. "That's right, if I do say so myself."

"Since time immemorial," Mr. Hale pointed out, "monsters have been attracting tourists!"

Go, Dad! Cornelia thought. *You tell him!*

The owner scowled. "You wouldn't be insinuating that I made up the whole story, would you?" he asked.

"Mr. Krinkle, I never insinuate," replied Mr. Hale.

No, you tell the truth, like I do, Cornelia added silently. She liked to think that she'd inherited her dad's honesty. Like him, she was down-to-earth – literally! After all, she had power over the earth!

"Good!" said Mr. Krinkle. He stood there for a minute, at a loss for words, and finally said, "Well, I'm off. Tonight we're holding a festival by the lake, and you're all invited!" As he headed for the door, he adjusted a picture on the wall and whispered to Lilian, "Bring a camera with you! Maybe you'll spot something!"

"Wow!" breathed Lilian. She seemed to be becoming more curious than scared. "A real monster!"

Once Mr. Krinkle had left, Cornelia went upstairs with her bags. She dumped them on the floor of a small bedroom near the stairs and lay down on the bed.

We've only been here five minutes and I'm ready to go home, she thought. It's going to be a really long week if I have to put up with Lilian's nonsense on top of everything else.

She could hear Sandra Doubman in the

bathroom, no doubt applying yet another layer of make-up. Then she heard her mum walk downstairs and ask her dad, "Not that these monster stories worry me, but where's Cornelia?"

"She's with that other monster," her dad said. "Your high-school friend."

Cornelia smiled to herself. He's got that right, she thought.

Her father did an impression of Sandra. *"Daahling! My reservations at the spa fell through! Could you put me up for just a little while?"* His voice was whiny and nasal, just like hers.

"You wouldn't be *insinuating* that she set all of this up so she'd be asked to stay?" her mum responded huffily.

Up in her bedroom, Cornelia silently came to her dad's defense. Nobody's insinuating anything, she told her mum in her mind. Dad's telling it like it is. The woman is a total user!

"As I told Krinkle," Mr. Hale said loftily, "I never insinuate. I make direct accusations!"

"Harold, how could you?" Cornelia's mum said in a tight voice. "Sandra Doubman has never been a leech!"

Mr. Hale seemed determined to make his point. "First, the ride over here," he said. "And now this! People change, Elizabeth!"

"Physically," said her mum firmly, "but not in character."

Cornelia thought it over. *Do* people change? she wondered. I guess I have.

It was getting hard for her to remember what she'd been like before W.I.T.C.H. Back then, she'd been a popular girl with everything going her way.

Things are still going my way, she thought. I have the best friends anyone could ask for. But I'm different . . . stronger, I guess.

She considered her best friends one by one. Will and Irma, Taranee, and Hay Lin.

Really, the same is true for all of us, she decided. They haven't fallen in love and lost it, the way I have. But none of us are the people we used to be. I can't decide if that's a good thing or a bad thing. We're growing up. That's what happens to people our age! For us, it's happening a little faster, because of W.I.T.C.H. But nobody remains clueless forever.

Like all of her thoughts, this one eventually turned to Caleb. Had he changed, too? Cornelia wondered. Candracar was different from Meridian. He could let his guard down there a little, since he was not hunted by Phobos's men. Cornelia hated to ask herself the next question, but she couldn't help it. Had his feelings for her changed along with the scenery? Did he still love her the way she loved him?

She didn't have any answers. And she wasn't sure she wanted any more questions, either.

It's definitely stuffy in here, she thought. I need some fresh air.

Cornelia got up off the bed and headed downstairs. Napoleon! she suddenly thought. She found his carrier in the kitchen and opened the door to let him out. He raced through the kitchen, quickly pushed the back door open with his nose, and bounded across the sweeping expanse of the backyard. Cornelia followed him a little way, then stood back and let him run. She could see her dad's point about leaving the city entirely behind. Here, Cornelia couldn't hear her neighbours or the whine of traffic. The only sounds were of birds chirping and of water lapping at the shore of the lake.

Cornelia was watching Napoleon romp when suddenly she realised she wasn't alone.

Sandra Doubman had crept up behind her, and Cornelia couldn't tell if Sandra was watching the cat or watching her.

"Ah! The lake!" Sandra cried. "Let me tell you about the time that your mother and I . . ."

Cornelia backed away from her and toward the house, but Sandra followed her.

She won't leave me alone, Cornelia thought. And now I can't grab Napoleon.

True to his nature, he was running as far away from Sandra as he could. Napoleon *was* an excellent judge of character.

Through the open window, Cornelia could hear her mum, still talking to her dad. Now, at last, her mum conceded a point. "I must admit I do find Sandra just a bit . . . different." Cornelia knew Sandra couldn't hear this conversation over the sound of her own voice.

She may be different from the way she used to be, I guess, Cornelia thought, but she's also different from other people. Suddenly she found Sandra more than just annoying . . . she found her creepy. Cornelia wasn't sure what Sandra could do to her, exactly, but she made a resolution on the spot: I have got to watch out for that woman.

NINE

Perfect! I've got her just where I want her, Luba, disguised as Sandra, gloated. Cornered on the holiday retreat! She has no clue how close to danger she is.

She and Cornelia were standing in front of the house, and Luba was spinning another tale about a time she'd spent with Cornelia's mother long ago. Her ability to read Mrs. Hale's memories had come in handy! As she dragged out her story, however, Luba was inwardly plotting her next move. After all, she had waited all this time to trap the Herald of Candracar. She couldn't mess up now.

This is where Caleb will find her, she thought, as she surveyed her surroundings. The location could not have been more auspicious. There was the lake, with a boat peacefully bobbing on its surface in the distance. There were gardens and trees and rolling hills. What's missing? Luba asked herself. People! Which made it the perfect place for a private rendezvous between the two young lovers. The perfect place for Luba to carry out her plan!

Luba crossed her arms and glanced quickly at her watch. He should be here soon, she thought. He will not be able to hold out much longer. Luba was counting on the one thing she knew to be true about Caleb: he would never come to earth without visiting Cornelia. While his official business was to capture Luba and bring her back to Candracar, Luba was absolutely certain he would sneak in a side trip to the girl he loved.

And then, Luba thought, I shall strike! Cornelia is my lure, and this isolated spot is the perfect cover for my attack.

Since Luba couldn't pinpoint the time when Caleb would arrive, however, she didn't want to let the girl out of her sight. In "Sandra's" uncomfortable high heels, Luba tottered after Cornelia, who was searching for Napoleon. The beast had once again fled from the Guardian, who pursued him with fierce dedication.

"I'm sorry," said Cornelia to the person she thought was Sandra Doubman, "but I'm afraid my cat doesn't care for your . . . um . . . company."

"That's strange," Luba drawled in her Sandra voice. "Animals usually adore me!"

Cornelia obviously cared more for the cat than for her mother's friend. "As long as you're around me," Cornelia said accusingly, "he'll keep running away!"

Luba could not show her anger . . . or frustration; the real Sandra would never have lost her temper. She waved her hand in the general direction of the cat and said, "Then run along and get him! I'll stay here like a good girl!" Which, of course, she had no intention of doing.

She wants to get as far away from me as possible, Luba thought, panicking for a moment. What if she has uncovered my real identity?

Cornelia took off after the cat, cooing, "Come on, Napoleon! Come here, sweetie!"

The sweet tone of the Guardian's voice was enough to make Luba sick. But she could not risk leaving Cornelia unwatched. Keeping a comfortable distance, she followed her into the woods at the edge of the property. "Luba is here, my dear. Only steps away from you," she muttered softly. She would be ready to move in on Caleb the very moment he arrived.

Gazing up at the treetops, Luba found herself thinking about Candracar. Its stone pillars were taller than any trees, soaring amid the billowy clouds at the very centre of infinity. Its beautifully carved Temple was filled with pure air and bright light. The Elders of Candracar lived quietly, observing what happened in the universe around them – and when there were problems, those problems were resolved.

Until, of course, these Guardians were anointed, as Luba reminded herself. Since then she had seen a different side of Candracar – a Candracar governed by easily misled fools.

Luba still believed that order could be restored to Candracar if the Guardians were replaced. But Cornelia and Caleb had foiled her first attempt, and Luba still winced when she remembered the way her scheme had unraveled. It was her fault, yes, that all five of the powers had ended up in Cornelia's hands. But what the girl had done with the magic was simply inexcusable. She had transferred those powers to the boy she thought she loved. She had revived a Murmurer, a deadly enemy of Candracar – within the Temple itself!

So Luba had put the girl on trial, and she had all but persuaded the Council of her guilt! But then, just as the sentence was about to be handed down, the Murmurer – Caleb – had pleaded with the Oracle. He'd offered himself as a servant to the Oracle, in exchange for letting his girlfriend have her powers again and resume her role as a Guardian. And the Oracle had agreed to it! Luba's blood still boiled at the memory. The Oracle had permitted Caleb's sacrifice. He had permitted Cornelia and her friends to go free.

The last thing Luba clearly remembered of Candracar was stepping between Caleb and Cornelia. "I will not allow it!" she had bellowed. But Caleb possessed a copy of the five powers now, and the Murmurer had used those very powers against her! Luba had been thrown to the floor, humiliated before the Council. After that, she realised, there was only one way for her to restore her dignity – and that was to leave the place altogether. She had fled.

Luba set her jaw in determination. Now, she thought, Caleb is hunting me down, and soon he'll find me, right here beside his beloved. When that happens, I'll change from the hunted into the hunter!

From out of the corner of her eye, Luba saw Cornelia looking in her direction, so she quickly pasted a smile on her – no, on Sandra's! – face. Cornelia had caught her cat, and now she held him up to the sky, singing, *"Gotcha!"* and dancing among the trees.

When the cat caught a glimpse of Luba's face, he screeched, leaped out of Cornelia's arms, and fled back toward the trees. Cornelia giggled and set off again after him, her long purple skirt billowing behind her.

Perhaps the real Sandra Doubman would find it charming to see the girl frolic with her pet, thought Luba. But I find it utterly disgusting!

That has been the problem with Guardians from the beginning, Luba thought. They are too young. They are carefree and irresponsible. They don't understand the importance of their power or the weight of their responsibility. Thankfully, she recalled, they will not be around for much longer. They will be free to laugh and frolic here on earth, as they have always done. But they will never again set foot in Candracar! Their magic will be removed and their shoes filled by more mature Guardians, who are truly worthy of their title.

I'll capture the young Herald, Luba vowed. I'll use his powers against the five Guardians! I don't want to destroy them. No, I just want to show the Oracle that they are unfit and incapable – once and for all. Luba clenched her fist and shook it at the trees, Sandra Doubman's bracelets clanking on her wrist.

And when that has occurred, she promised herself, I will return to Candracar once again, my head held high!

TEN

The bus turned cautiously down a shady lane and shivered to a stop in the centre of town. Will sprang out of her seat and stretched her arms toward the ceiling. Then she put on her striped blue sweater and headed down the aisle, motioning for Caleb to follow.

I seriously thought I was going to be sick if I had to sit there another minute, Will thought. From her seat in the back, she had felt every bump in the road and breathed in all the fumes the bus belched out. Caleb was captivated by the scenery, but Will hadn't been as impressed.

It's new and different to him, she thought, but after a while it all starts to look the same to me. Thank goodness we're here!

The only thing better than getting off the bus would have been meeting up with her friends at last. Will was starting to feel a familiar knot in her stomach, and she knew that it would only go away when they had united to find Luba and Cornelia.

First things first, she told herself. Let's get our bearings and find out where the Hales are staying.

Will didn't know which way to go, but she figured it was a safe bet to follow the other passengers through the stone archway that opened off the main street.

Will stepped through it and squinted in the bright light. She was in a narrow street that was lined with shops and seemed totally off limits to cars. The street was so steep that there were stairs instead of sidewalks! At the bottom, Will could see the magnificent Riddlescott Lake, dotted with boats and gleaming in the afternoon sun. The village of Riddlescott stretched along the shoreline, its charming old houses painted in pastel colours. Will couldn't help thinking that the buildings looked like candies in a box. She'd heard kids at school talking about Riddlescott Lake, and now she knew why. It was absolutely breathtaking.

Leave it to the Hales to pick such a nice place for their trip, she thought. She knew that her vacation with her mum wouldn't be anything like that. That is, if I ever make it there, Will added in her mind.

Her thoughts leaped suddenly to Astral Will, back home in Heatherfield with her mum and Mr. Collins.

How's she doing? Will wondered. Does she have them convinced she's me? Will always felt nervous leaving an astral drop behind, but she tried to banish all worry from her mind just then. This was a place where people took it easy, she told herself. And she needed to take it easy, too! Irma, Hay Lin, and Taranee would be there soon, and then they could do what they had to do.

The redhead stopped to read a sign in front of a sunglasses shop. It said: *Welcome to Riddlescott! Our lovely town lies on the lake named after it. It thrives on fishing.*

When Will noticed Caleb reading over her shoulder, she said drily, "Fishing for tourists, obviously."

As they made their way down the stairs in

the direction of the lake, Will noticed something strange. Many of the shop windows displayed photos of a creature that looked sort of like a dinosaur. The name Scotty was displayed underneath many of them. What's that supposed to be? Will wondered. Some kind of monster?

Her thoughts were interrupted when a bearded man jumped out from behind a parked car. "Pssstt! Hey, kids!" he hissed.

"Huh? Who, us?" Will said to the man. She was totally confused. She was in no mood to chat.

Caleb had been looking in the other direction, shielding his eyes from the sun and regarding the view. Suddenly, though, he was glued to Will's side.

The man came closer to the two of them, rubbing his chin. Will took him to be a local, what with his overalls and his fisherman's cap.

"I've seen him, you know! I've seen Scotty, the lake monster!" the man declared.

"What do you say to that?" Caleb muttered under his breath.

"I say he wants to sell us something," Will muttered back. A bunch of brochures were sticking out of the back pocket of the guy's overalls. Something wasn't right.

The guy waggled his finger in the air and said, "I know this lake like the back of my hand! Come here!" He whipped around, opened the door of the parked car, and gestured for them to climb in after him.

"Not on your life!" Will wanted to say. She was getting a bad vibe. Did this guy have anything to do with Luba? she wondered. Where did he really want to take them?

"Keep your eyes open!" the man warned. "I don't believe in fairy tales, and I'm just an elderly fisherman, but . . ."

He was interrupted by an old woman walking by. "Hello there, Mayor Krinkle!" she said cheerfully. "Are you going to a costume party?"

Will's heart started beating a little slower. He was the mayor? she thought. In disguise? It didn't make any sense, but whatever. At least he wasn't going to hurt them.

Will turned to Caleb and rolled her eyes. What a weirdo! All along the guy had just been doing the public-relations thing. Suddenly it seemed ridiculous that she'd been scared.

"You were saying?" she asked Mayor

Krinkle with a smug smirk.

He looked annoyed as he peeled off his fake beard. "I just wanted to wish you a nice stay and give you this guide to the area." He plucked a brochure from his pocket and pushed it into Will's hands. Then he stalked off, pausing to remove his overalls right there in the street. Luckily, another pair of pants was revealed.

She followed him and asked, "Don't we owe you anything for the guide?"

The mayor muttered, "If I were that fisherman, you bet I'd sell it to you! But as the mayor I have to give it to you for free."

The guide might come in handy, Will thought. Especially if it had a map. They still didn't know where to go.

Then she started thinking. This guy's the mayor, she realised. Maybe he can help us! "We're looking for our friends from Heatherfield!" she shouted before he passed out of earshot. "The Hale family!"

The mayor stopped short and came back to answer her. "I rented them a nice house not too far from here," he said, sounding more friendly. "You want me to call them for you?"

Will caught Caleb's eye and gave him a

quick thumbs-up. "Actually, I think we'd rather surprise them," she said casually.

"Then come to the town festival on the side of the lake tonight!" suggested the mayor. "They'll be there, for sure!" Without another word, he walked away.

Will was glad to see him disappear into the distance, carrying his disguise. She was grateful for the information, too. There was only one big problem now. Hay Lin, Irma, and Taranee still hadn't shown up, so they wouldn't know to look for Will and Caleb.

Will looked at her watch for the umpteenth time. Where were they? she wondered. Had something happened?

She studied the mayor's brochure, not knowing what else to do.

"So, what's planned for the festival?" Caleb asked.

"Well, our plan is to get near Cornelia without making Luba suspicious," Will responded. She was supposed to be leading the way, but she felt as if they'd come to a roadblock. Without her friends, she didn't know which way to turn. "But maybe we should wait until the others get here," she added.

Caleb's expression grew serious. "We have to do something *tonight*, Will," he said with conviction. "Who knows if we'll get another chance?"

He was right. They couldn't waste any time. And Will wasn't really alone if she had Caleb by her side. After all, she remembered, he was with me the minute the mayor started in with his crazy story. He's been absorbing and observing everything he sees. Nobody cares more about this mission than he does! We'll just have to go ahead.

Will knew she couldn't handle the situation alone. With Caleb, though, she had a chance. "Whatever you say, Caleb," she assented. "Let's go!" She clutched her brochure and gazed longingly into the distance. "I just hope those friends of mine get here quick!"

ELEVEN

Sitting on the curb outside the Green Bay bus station, Hay Lin hugged her knees to her chest. She glanced over at Irma, then averted her eyes immediately. Hay Lin could almost feel the rays of anger coming off her friend, like heat from the sun. It was dangerous to stare at the sun – and it was clearly dangerous to stare at Irma, too!

This isn't really like her, Hay Lin thought. Yeah, she blows up sometimes. But this time she's just simmering, like the pots of soup Dad keeps on the back burner at the restaurant.

Hay Lin wanted to help her friend turn down the heat, but she had a feeling she'd have to wait.

Hay Lin got up and went to

check the bus schedule posted outside the station, hoping she might see something different this time. But the next bus was still not due for two whole hours. Will's got to be in Riddlescott by now, Hay Lin figured. The first thing she'll do is find Cornelia and Luba. And that's where the rest of us will come in, except that Irma and I will be just getting on the bus when Will needs us. That's what has Irma so annoyed.

But Hay Lin was determined to look on the bright side.

It was easier said than done. The bus station was dingy and deserted. The vending machines were empty, and the only newspapers for sale were those of the previous day. Nobody would have guessed that this was a popular beach town if they stood there, Hay Lin thought. Unless they happened to look up and spot the palm trees in the parking lot. That might have given it away.

Back when our vacation started, the bus station was the last place I'd have thought we'd end up! Hay Lin thought. But she was starting to realise there was only one rule for being in W.I.T.C.H. right now: expect the unexpected.

When they'd all arrived in Green Bay for

the weeklong vacation at Irma's, Hay Lin was happy that her best friends were relaxing together for the first time in forever. But then she'd catch Cornelia staring into space and she knew that Caleb was still on her mind. Or she'd wake up in the middle of the night and hear Will murmuring, half asleep, as if somebody were making threats in her dreams. Hay Lin's friends might have acted all close and carefree, but she could tell they were secretly distracted . . . and freaked out. It felt as though Nerissa were everywhere!

Then, when Hay Lin was taking a walk on the beach, she'd fallen into a mysterious sinkhole in the sand. Her friends had been able to pull her out – just in time to save her from a scary guy in armor, who was trying to grab her foot. Someone was after her. Someone was after *all of them*!

Hay Lin's grandmother had been the one to tell them all about Nerissa.

Yan Lin warned the girls that it was just a matter of time before Nerissa was on their trail. Nerissa would stop at nothing to get the Heart of Candracar back.

So what did this all mean for Hay Lin? It

meant that she had to watch her step and stick with her friends, for one thing. But it also meant something bigger. It meant that *nothing* was back to normal – no matter how much she wanted it to be.

Hay Lin sighed and smiled.

I'm not going to let that get me down, she vowed. It's just lucky my power is over air. I'm used to flying on the breeze, letting it take me where it goes. With W.I.T.C.H., I just need to hang on for the ride!

Her long black pigtails bouncing, Hay Lin walked back to the curb and sat back down next to Irma. "What a disaster," her friend moaned. "What a big, fat, hairy disaster!"

At least she's talking, Hay Lin thought. Things are looking up! She waited for Irma to go on.

"And to think that I was the one who came up with Operation E.G.A.D., Emergency Group Astral Drops. What was I thinking?" Irma buried her face in her hands.

"Well, at least part of it worked," Hay Lin said optimistically. "Will called, then we created two doubles of ourselves. Those astral drops replaced us so that we could sneak away and get to the bus station, no problem!" Hay Lin swept her hand out in front of her, indicating their lovely surroundings. Irma let out a groan.

They'd gotten Will's call while they were still at Irma's. Or Irma's dad had gotten the call, to be more exact – Will's message said only that they should call her back. Hay Lin and Irma had scrambled to find a pay phone at Camp Cormoran so that they could speak in private, and when they finally got in touch, Will filled them in on the whole story. Cornelia and Caleb. Luba and Riddlescott Lake. That was all they needed to know.

Creating astral drops had always made Hay Lin a little nervous, ever since they had discovered the trick. There was the chance of getting caught in two places at once, and she and her friends hadn't had the best luck in the past. Once, Irma had gotten trapped in her astral form, and another time, Will's astral drop had kissed Will's crush, Matt! (A major no-no, since he wasn't supposed to know she liked him.)

But this time, everything seemed to be working out right. The girls had called up their magic, and it had swirled around them like a rainbow-coloured tornado. When the magical storm subsided, the girls' twins had been standing next to them. The real Hay Lin and Irma had snuck out of the cabin as quickly as they could.

"Yeah, we made it just in time for the Riddlescott Lake Express," Irma muttered, bringing Hay Lin back to the present. "That is, just in time to miss it!"

As if on cue, a bus pulled out of the station and roared away, trailing exhaust. "There it goes, leaving without us!" Irma pointed out.

Hay Lin wrapped an arm around Irma and gave her a quick squeeze. "Come on, Irma! Cheer up!" she said. "It's not like we technically missed it. Everyone forgets their bus fare once in a while!"

It's just a *mistake*, Hay Lin thought. Get over it already!

There was only so much cheering up she could do.

Irma rested her chin in her hand glumly. "Yeah, yeah, everyone forgets," she said. Then she snapped, "But it shouldn't be us! Now we have to catch a later bus!"

Hay Lin shrugged as if to say, "It's not the end of the world." We just have to hope that we get there before Will really needs us, Hay Lin added to herself.

Apparently, not having the bus fare wasn't the only thing bothering Irma. "Now we have to go back to the cabin and get some cash," she grumbled.

"And risk being seen together with our twins!" Hay Lin chimed in. That part of it bothered her, too. She was as worried about getting caught as Irma. Anyway, Irma's parents were probably on the beach. The girls would be in and out of the cabin in a flash.

"Thanks for reminding me, Hay Lin," Irma said.

"No sweat, Irma!" Hay Lin giggled. "Let's just hope that Taranee is having better luck. Sesamo is pretty far from Riddlescott, and Taranee said she was going to take the train." If Hay Lin was guessing right, Taranee would barely have made it to the mountain village of Sesamo when she'd get Will's call and have to leave again.

Taranee should be in Riddlescott by now, Hay Lin thought. And at least that will even out the numbers a little. Two of them there and two of us, well, running a little late.

Silently, Hay Lin followed Irma out of the station. As they passed a line of taxis, she almost suggested hopping in one, but then she thought better of it.

We have two hours to kill before the next bus, Hay Lin remembered. We might as well get some exercise!

The Lairs were nowhere in sight when the girls arrived back at the cabin. Hay Lin hid in some bushes and kept watch while Irma went inside to find her money. Hay Lin tried not to think about the guy with the hatchets who'd been stalking them the first night they were at Camp Cormoran. He'd disappeared when the girls confronted him on the beach, a day later. But where was he now? Hay Lin wondered. He had Nerissa's sign on his chest, and that couldn't be good. Hay Lin was pretty sure he wasn't there just then, but she wished she knew for certain.

Suddenly Irma came outside, waving some money in one hand and giving Hay Lin a thumbs-up with another. When Irma bought them each a smoothie and led the way back to the station, Hay Lin knew the earlier bad mood was gone.

Soon they had forgotten all about the

missing bus fare. They walked through town, doing a little window-shopping. When Hay Lin looked at her watch a while later, she gasped. They had to get going! If they missed *this* bus, they were sunk.

Hay Lin watched nervously as Irma walked up to the ticket counter. Their bus was idling in the lot, and there wasn't a moment to lose. Hay Lin caught Irma's eye after a few minutes had passed, and Irma pointed to the ticket window. The agent inside had disappeared with her money.

"How long is this going to take?" Hay Lin wondered, tapping her foot on the ground. "We're way late!" Her laid-back attitude was starting to fade away.

Just then, a group of people walked past the station. She did a double take and gulped. Tell me this is just a bad dream! Hay Lin said to herself.

It was the entire Lair family, coming her way – with Irma's astral drop! They were eating ice cream and chatting at the moment, but all they needed to do was turn their heads a little and the girls' cover would be blown. Irma's astral drop was wearing a red-and-white-striped sleeveless top with jeans rolled halfway up to her knees. The Lairs would definitely wonder why there was another Irma buying a ticket at the bus station *and* wearing the exact same outfit, right down to the sweater tied around her waist!

Hay Lin quickly turned around, hoping they wouldn't see her. She overheard Sergeant Lair say to Astral Irma, "Hey, I think I'll just stop by the station and check out the timetable. Want to come with me?"

"Sure, Dad," chirped Astral Irma. The two of them headed toward the ticket window. The real Irma's ticket window!

Meanwhile, Irma was still waiting – she had no idea what was about to happen. The ticket agent had finally returned to the window. He was extremely old, and his voice was slow. "Just another second, young lady," he croaked. "I still need to get your change."

"Aw, take your time," Irma said flippantly. "I'll just wait here and miss the bus all over again!"

Hay Lin stole another look at Sergeant Lair and Astral Irma. They were still several feet away, and luckily they were busy looking at something in the other direction.

I have to warn Irma, Hay Lin decided. Even if they see me.

She raced toward her friend, waving her arms in the air, loudly whispering, "Irma! They're heading right for us! They're . . ."

She didn't have a chance to finish her sentence, because suddenly something strange started happening. One minute Hay Lin's hands were right in front of her, flailing about wildly. Then, one by one, they disappeared – just dropped out of sight as if they'd been snapped off. But Hay Lin could still feel them, so she knew they weren't really gone. It's just that they were . . . invisible. But I didn't do any magic! Hay Lin thought. She was totally confused. And before she could figure it out, the rest of her body started disappearing, too. The only evidence that she'd ever been at the bus station was her smoothie cup, sticking out of the trash.

The next thing she knew, Hay Lin was rocketing across Green Bay, high up in the air, some magnetic force whisking her to who knew where.

Is somebody calling me to Candracar? Hay Lin wondered. Or is this Nerissa's doing? A jolt of pure fear shot through her body like a bolt of lightning . . . and then she realised that Irma was invisible, too, and along for the ride. She couldn't see Irma, of course, but she could sense her. There was just something about the energy in the air. . . .

Suddenly, Hay Lin couldn't help laughing. "I just wish I could see what's happening at the bus station right now!" she giggled. The ancient ticket agent would be shuffling back to the window, but Irma would be gone. Just in time for Astral Irma to take her place! None the wiser, the agent would blink and say, "Ah, there you are! Well, here's your change. Have a nice trip, now!"

It made Hay Lin feel a lot better to know that Irma was nearby. She remembered what she'd been thinking back at the bus station: *we have to expect the unexpected with W.I.T.C.H.*

TWELVE

Taranee walked into the Sesamo train station. A schedule was posted on the station wall, and Taranee checked it again, just to be sure. With one finger she found Sesamo on the schedule; with the other she found Riddlescott. Just as I thought, she confirmed to herself. The train doesn't leave for fifteen minutes. Plenty of time to buy my ticket.

From the last time she'd been in Sesamo with her family, Taranee remembered that several train lines ran through the town. I need to find a map, she realised, to figure out which one goes to Riddlescott. She walked out onto the train platform and found the map mounted in a glass case there.

Taranee looked at the train routes in their different colours, crisscrossing the countryside. Then she figured out which line she would need to take, the kind of ticket she would need to buy, and how many stops the train would make before it pulled into Riddlescott. Finally, she approached the ticket agent.

Some train stations had computerised machines that allowed you to purchase and print your own ticket – but not Sesamo. The tiny mountain town didn't have much in the way of modern conveniences, which was why Taranee's parents liked it so much.

Guess that's why there's only one person working here, Taranee thought.

A train thundered by as Taranee inched up in the line. Not too long ago, the noise of it would have freaked her out.

But I'm not such a scaredy-cat anymore, Taranee told herself proudly. I mean, check it out! I'm making this trip on my own.

After the adventures she'd had with W.I.T.C.H., taking a train alone – or seeing one zoom by – was no big deal at all. Taranee liked the way that W.I.T.C.H. had toughened her up. But sometimes she wondered how much more she could take. She'd seen and done a lot of things that would normally be hard for a girl her age. She was ready for a little peace and quiet, but she had a feeling she wasn't about to get it with Luba in Riddlescott.

How am I going to find my friends once I get there? she wondered. Even W.I.T.C.H. couldn't keep Taranee from being a worrywart. But her thoughts were interrupted when the ticket agent called out, "Next!"

Taranee smiled and handed the agent her money. "One ticket, please," she said.

The woman behind the counter put on her glasses and gave Taranee the once-over. "You're a minor, and you're travelling alone, young lady?" she asked, shaking her finger accusingly.

Since when is that a crime? Taranee wondered silently. "Oh, no," she replied, congratulating herself on her quick save. "My folks are with me, too. In fact, I need three tickets."

The next thing she knew, the woman had hoisted herself halfway out the ticket window! "I don't see anyone out there with you," she announced. "I bet you're a runaway!"

A nosy ticket lady. That's all I need, Taranee

thought. This was a complication she hadn't expected.

"Um, no! No!" she stammered. "I'll call my mum and dad! I'm not sure where they got off to, but I know they're around here somewhere. . . ." Taranee was still blathering on when a deep voice overpowered her own.

"Hey, you! Stop right there!" it said.

Taranee swallowed hard. The person speaking to her was a police officer, striding toward her with his partner. Now what do I do? she asked herself.

The officer put his hand on her shoulder and smoothly guided her inside the ticket office. The door closed behind her, and the officers flanked her. Taranee realised she couldn't escape. She *knew* what was coming. They were going to call her parents. They were going to ruin everything.

Figures! she thought. Everything had been going too smoothly.

Taranee had heard from Will the minute her family had arrived in Sesamo. They had still been unloading the car, in fact – which was why Taranee had happened to be alone in the house when the phone rang. She'd done an astral drop as soon as Will filled her in on what was happening. Plus, she figured it wouldn't hurt for her astral drop to be the one doing the heavy lifting of the luggage! But if the police called home, her parents would realise there were *two* Taranees at large. Taranee knew one person who wouldn't be happy: her mum.

Mrs. Cook was a judge in Heatherfield. Taranee knew a little more than she wanted to know about her mum's sense of justice, because her crush, shy Nigel, had crossed paths with her mum in court! He had been hanging with the wrong crowd and, when his friends got the crazy idea to sneak into the Heatherfield Museum after hours one night, he had gone along with it. At their sentencing, Judge Cook didn't come down *too* harshly on the boys. But she didn't let them off the hook, either – they'd been sentenced to cleaning the museum! Nigel didn't seem to hold it against Taranee, but his friends had not let her forget it.

And mum will never let me forget *this*, Taranee thought.

Her anxiety doubled when one of the policemen picked up a desk phone. Staring at her coldly, he asked for her phone number.

Taranee thought briefly about stalling and saying she didn't know the number where she was staying, but she decided to give them her mum's cell-phone number instead. If they couldn't reach her family by phone, she guessed that the next thing would be for them to drive her back – and she really didn't want to see her mum's face as she was told about what had happened. Taranee wondered what her astral drop was doing right at that moment. Unpacking? Reading on the deck? I'd do anything to trade places with her right now, Taranee thought.

The taller, thinner officer dialled the number, pursing his lips as he waited for an answer. Taranee had the feeling her mum was the one who picked up – whoever was on the other end of the line seemed to be all business. The policeman listened politely and, in response to some question, said, "Yes! Taranee Cook, around thirteen years old!"

The smaller, rounder officer tuned out. He turned to the ticket agent and said, "Thanks for letting us use your phone, ma'am!"

The ticket agent glared at Taranee, who was sitting miserably on a bench in the corner of the room. "Don't mention it!" she said. "My own daughter ran away from home once!"

With a mother like that, Taranee thought, who could blame her?

"I . . . I really need to step outside for a minute," she said to the officer. Maybe they'd let her get some fresh air on the platform?

The smaller policeman ushered her back to her seat. "Not so fast!" he said. "Sit down! You kids today are always in such a rush."

The taller officer was still on the phone. "I don't understand, Mrs. Cook," he said heatedly. "No, this is not a practical joke!"

Oh, I am so busted, Taranee thought. The next thing she knew, her mum would want to talk to her.

But she heard her mother's next words very clearly. Taranee could tell that her mum was making an effort to enunciate into the phone, the way she always reminded her kids to do. "My daughter is right here with me at this very moment! Have I made myself clear?"

Taranee was stunned. Her mum didn't believe the officer! Astral Taranee must be sitting right there, Taranee deduced. Amazing – the astral drop was actually working. She was doing a great job of filling in for Taranee! Why should Taranee's mum believe the policeman's story when evidence to the contrary was right in front of her? Taranee had never been so grateful that her mum always evaluated a problem by looking at the facts.

Saved by the drop! she rejoiced, looking at her watch. There was still a little time before the train to Riddlescott. This little detour wouldn't stop her from being there for her friends.

The taller policeman slammed down the phone, shaking his head. "How embarrassing!" he said. "Are you sure you got the girl's name right?" he asked his partner.

"Let's ask her for it again," the shorter officer replied. "I don't know. . . . Maybe I got it wrong."

Taranee was still waiting on the bench obediently. She was just sitting there, when suddenly she had the strangest sensation. It was as though she were being . . . erased. One minute she could see her feet planted on the floor beneath the bench, and the next minute they were gone. *She* was gone. Off and heading toward some unknown destination.

Taranee was glad to be out of the station, but a little disappointed that she couldn't see the ticket agent's reaction. She could just imagine the woman shaking as she screamed, "She . . . she disappeared! She was sitting there just a second ago!" And she could picture the shorter policeman scratching his head in confusion. "Like I said," he'd drawl, "kids today are always in a rush."

It occurred to Taranee that she should be scared.

I'm invisible, and I'm hurtling through the air, she thought. Not something that happens every day.

But for some reason she felt more curious than frightened.

This has got to be happening for a reason, Taranee thought. Maybe I'm on a mission and I don't even know it? Maybe I'll be with my friends when this is over. Maybe I'll be up against an enemy. Whatever it is, though, W.I.T.C.H. has made me brave. And wherever I land, I'm ready for action!

THIRTEEN

A full moon rose over Riddlescott Lake, bathing the town festival in light. Hundreds of stars twinkled in the clear sky, and a gentle breeze rippled the water without chilling the air.

Cornelia, holding Napoleon, followed her family to the end of a pier that was decorated with colourful lanterns and streamers. This spot offered the best view of the festival, from the big striped tent to the Ferris wheel and the merry-go-round. Cornelia could hear the cheerful music being played by roving musicians. She could see the throngs of happy vacationers lining up to buy ice cream and cotton candy from friendly vendors. She could even see a neon Scotty sign perched above a makeshift restaurant.

Everyone else seemed enchanted by the fair, but Cornelia secretly thought it was a little hokey.

It's all so perfect, she thought, from the old-fashioned games to the wholesome treats. Has this really been an annual tradition for the last hundred years, like the mayor says? Or is he just trying to make it seem that way?

Cornelia was used to Heatherfield, where every event was crowded and chaotic.

That's what I love about the city, she thought. You never know who's going to show up for things. You never know what's going to happen.

The Riddlescott festival, on the other hand, seemed tightly controlled. Suddenly Cornelia felt very far from home.

I'm a city girl at heart, she decided. I feel too big for this place already!

Clearly, her parents didn't share her point of view. Their arms were linked as they gazed around. Cornelia was happy they were so relaxed, but seeing them all lovey-dovey also set off a familiar ache in her heart.

Oh, Caleb, she thought, her eyes filling with tears. When will I get to see you again?

She tried to remember what it felt like to be close to the boy she loved. But her precious memories were shattered by the shrill voice of her little sister. "Mummy! Daddy! I put three chocolate cookies on the pier!"

"What for, Lilian?" asked Mrs. Hale.

Lilian clasped her hands together hopefully. "So Scotty the monster will come and eat them! That way I can take his picture!"

Cornelia's dad smiled. "I bet it was Mayor Krinkle who suggested that trick!" he said.

"Yeah! He even gave me the cookies!" Lilian boasted, pointing to a brightly lit tent in the centre of the fair.

How did I miss it before? Cornelia wondered. The mayor was working in the booth himself, selling Scotty-shaped cookies. To judge by the piles of cookies and the length of the line, there was a huge demand. All because Mayor Krinkle had been telling people lies, Cornelia thought, frowning.

She was totally fed up with her lovey-dovey parents and her gullible sister. She was sick of Riddlescott's quaint country charm – and she'd only just arrived.

I need a little space, Cornelia thought.

Maybe I'll wander through the fair to see if I've missed anything cool, then head back to the house. Nobody will worry about me in this village – they'll know to meet me at home.

Cornelia squeezed Napoleon as she walked back along the pier. She stroked his fur and scratched his ears.

You're the only one I can deal with right now, she thought. You're the only one who never gets on my nerves.

Turning a corner and walking past a ring-toss booth, Cornelia spotted Sandra Doubman in the crowd. She managed to avoid making eye contact, but she still had a creepy feeling that Sandra had noticed her walking by. "There she is!" Cornelia said quietly to her cat. "It's almost as if she's following me!"

Yes, she thought wryly. It is officially impossible for me to be alone.

Looking on the bright side, Cornelia felt grateful that at least Sandra hadn't bounced over to her with yet another story about the time when she was young.

She's only keeping her distance because I'm holding Napoleon, she realised. She knows the cat will scratch her if I let him out of my arms.

So if I keep him with me . . .

Suddenly Napoleon began squirming like crazy in Cornelia's arms. The next thing she knew, he had wriggled out of her grasp and run away – straight into the surrounding woods!

"You little rascal!" Cornelia shouted. "You're starting to make running away a habit!" She didn't want to lose him in a place he didn't know, so she took off after him. He'd probably be able to find his way home, but Cornelia wasn't taking any chances.

Napoleon was running at top speed, and soon the fair was just a distant blur of light and sound. Cornelia couldn't see the cat anymore, since it was dark amid the trees. Still, she figured Napoleon was nearby because she heard rustling in the leaves. "Do you want both of us to get lost in this forest?" Cornelia cried.

Suddenly the leaves stopped rustling. Cornelia grew still so she could hear Napoleon's next move. But he didn't stir. Instead, he started purring!

That's strange, Cornelia thought. She stepped into a clearing and saw Napoleon in the moonlight. He was lying on his back, his four legs in the air. He was purring because his tummy was being scratched. Cornelia's heart leaped into her throat when she saw a figure beside Napoleon in the shadows. And then she realised it was someone she knew.

"Will!" Cornelia cried. "What on earth?" She had never been so glad to see a friend in her life.

Will put a finger to her lips. "Shhh!" she whispered. "Follow me, and don't ask any questions. We have to get away from here, quick!"

Silently, Cornelia followed her friend deeper into the woods.

Will must have planned this, Cornelia realised. She must have lured Napoleon to her, hoping I would follow.

Forgetting she was supposed to be quiet, Cornelia blurted out, "I don't get it! How did you manage to get Napoleon to come to you?"

Napoleon was still purring in Will's arms. "You can communicate with plants," Will said matter-of-factly, "and I can do the same with animals!"

The last I heard, Cornelia thought, Will could only talk to electrical appliances! Maybe she has acquired new powers. It's totally like her to keep a power like this to herself. Will doesn't brag about her magic. That's why she's always full of surprises.

"Why did you come all the way to Riddlescott?" Cornelia whispered. "Is there some kind of emergency?"

Will pointed to a figure half hidden behind a tree. "Don't ask me. Ask him!" she said with a knowing smile.

The person stepped toward Cornelia, a gust of wind blowing some leaves around his head. It was the best surprise that Cornelia could imagine. *It was Caleb!*

She felt as if a switch had been thrown on and a current had begun to flow again within her heart.

He's here! she rejoiced. On earth!

She didn't know the reason for his visit, and she didn't care. Caleb's blue eyes bored into hers as he slowly moved toward her. Cornelia was speechless – and so was he.

When he was right beside her, Caleb bent his head and put his hands up in front of him. Cornelia raised her hands, too, and touched her fingertips to his. His fingers felt so soft and warm, so kind and familiar, she thought. So right! Cornelia tilted her face and moved her lips closer to Caleb's. She closed her eyes and prepared for the sweetest moment of her life since that terrible day when she'd left Candracar, and . . .

Shaarz!

Caleb was zapped by a beam of light! His face contorted in pain, and he fell to the ground, moaning.

NO! Cornelia thought. Not again!

She knelt and bent over him, her tears falling on his shiny dark hair as she stroked his forehead. "Caleb!" she cried. "What happened? Are you all right?" His body was warm but motionless.

Why? she thought. Why are we doomed every step of the way?

From the corner of her eye she saw Will move among the shadows of the trees. A cloud had covered the moon, making the forest pitch-black. When it blew away, however, the shimmering light fell on an all-too-familiar, long, white robe. Cornelia blinked to make sure she was seeing correctly. The robe belonged to Luba, the cat-woman from Candracar, who totally had it in for her.

What's she doing here? Cornelia thought in panic.

"Caleb is in my power now," Luba announced gravely. "He can hear and see, but he cannot reply."

Cornelia's face grew red with rage. "What did he ever do to you?" she wanted to scream. Sure, Caleb had messed up Luba's plan to take away the girls' powers and replace the Guardians with a new set of people, Cornelia remembered. But does she hold such a grudge that she has to come to earth to kick Caleb one more time?

The blonde Guardian struggled for something to say. "You?" she finally asked. She was too stunned to form coherent sentences.

Luba smiled, exposing two neat rows of pointy cat teeth. "You don't know how difficult it was to stay close to you, daahling!" she snickered. It was a familiar voice, Cornelia realised. Sandra's voice!

Cornelia felt as though her brain were underwater.

So Luba disguised herself as Sandra? she thought slowly. She was following me to get to Caleb? But how did she know he was coming here?

"Sandra!" Cornelia snapped. "It can't be! How could I not have noticed . . ."

Then there was a sharp sound from the forest, almost like a shot. Cornelia couldn't see what it was or where it came from, but suddenly Luba threw her hands up in the air, whirled around, and plummeted face-first to the forest floor.

Her back was blazing where a shaft of orange light had blasted her robe and pierced the iridescent cloth.

As Cornelia watched, transfixed with terror, the beam turned to flames, which burned a neat circle on Luba's back and slashed the circle through with a lightning bolt. When the flames finished branding Luba, they vanished as quickly as they'd appeared. Soon all Cornelia could see were two small puffs of smoke where the fire had been – and the mark of Nerissa, staring defiantly at her from the back of Luba's robe.

FOURTEEN

Will hid in the shadows for a second, trying to collect her thoughts. Luba had hurt Caleb, but *somebody else* had hurt Luba.

Was it Cornelia? Will wondered for a second. She had an obvious motive, Will thought, her eyes jumping to where Caleb's body still lay. But the sign of Nerissa, burnt into Luba's robe, suggested that larger forces were at work.

The smell of singed fur wafted in Will's direction from Luba's body, which remained motionless in the grass between two trees. Was Luba dead? Will wondered. At least in the trees she had a little protection. From whatever, or whomever, was out there.

Suddenly, something rustled close

to Will's head. She whipped around, but couldn't see anything in the darkness. Then she craned her neck toward the sky . . . and there they were.

Two huge figures hovered in the air, partially transparent and larger than life.

One was a winged woman with hair standing straight up on her head like a bunch of flames. She wore a short dress, edged in metal, and tall boots. In her hand she carried a lethal-looking double-sided spear, and her large, red eyes glowed in the dark. Her glare was focused right on Will.

The woman's travelling companion was a muscle-bound blue guy with wings like an eagle's and a shield that covered only his torso. His huge arms and legs were free to crush anyone who crossed his path. His head was hairless, but his eyebrows were thick, making his stare look all the more threatening, and he was holding a deadly hatchet.

It looks like I could stick my hand right through them, Will thought. Are they ghosts? she wondered, her pulse racing. Do they talk?

"Nerissa was right!" the woman hissed to the man. "Find the Keeper of the Aurameres, and you'll find the Herald as well!" Will could see the woman's attention shift to Caleb, a short distance away.

"Now we simply have to do away with these little girls!" the man roared in reply.

Nerissa sent them, Will told herself. And we don't know how to fight Nerissa! Last time we met one of Nerissa's beasts it almost took us out – and we were *all* together. What can Cornelia and I do?

Cornelia, however, seemed distracted by the way the monsters were talking about Caleb.

"Hear that, Will?" Cornelia asked angrily. "Miss Nightmare has sent us two new beasts!"

Cornelia's tone snapped Will right out of her panic. "Yeah, well, I guess we'll have to mark them 'Return to Sender'!" Will yelled. "I'd say it's time for a transformation!" Their friends might have been missing, but Will and Cornelia still had their magic.

The Heart of Candracar appeared in the palm of Will's hand, glowing like a star. She cupped her hands around it instinctively as she waited for the Heart to toss out tear-shaped droplets of pure magic, the way it always did.

The blue guy crouched in midair, stretching

his thick arm toward the Heart. "Look! The Heart of Candracar! Let's get it!" he panted.

The red woman put her hand on his shoulder to hold him back. "Wait! We're not here for that now!"

Will's palm lit up in a blaze of pink light. She closed her eyes as the power of the Heart swirled all around her. Will loved that feeling – it was like being safe at the centre of the storm. It was like being herself on the best of all possible days. When she opened her eyes, Will had been transformed into her stronger, more magical form – with wings! Plus an outfit that made her feel as if she could handle anything.

But she couldn't think about the clothes just then! The blue guy was still obsessing about the Heart!

"What does it matter that we're not here to get it?" he argued with the woman. "Nerissa will be pleased if we do!"

The blue creature swung his hatchet toward Will and Cornelia, who danced away before it struck a tree with a deafening *kraaam!*

"Is that all you can do?" Cornelia taunted as the tree was split in half.

The blue guy's eyes narrowed hatefully as

he informed her of his name. "I am Tridart, you insolent child. The incarnation of desperation! I can do what I want."

Now the woman chimed in. "And if you want to know pain, meet me – Ember!" She lifted her spear and pointed it at Will.

The Guardian was not surprised to see it shoot flames. Now she knew for sure who'd brought Luba down. "What a happy little couple!" Will jeered. "Did your friends set you up on a blind date?"

Cornelia called up a magical barrier to block her and Will from Ember's flames. "We have to keep them away from Caleb! Give me a hand!" she whispered fiercely.

Will was moving toward Caleb when she was suddenly stopped by an intense sensation of burning in her palm. Without even knowing it, Will had clenched her hands into fists. And when she opened her left hand, the Heart of Candracar popped right out!

That's not supposed to happen, Will thought in alarm. We just used it. It should stay inside me until next time I call to it.

"Wait! The Heart is lighting up," she said to Cornelia. "What the . . ."

An image had appeared in the Heart's pink light. It was a picture of Caleb as he'd been on the bus to Riddlescott. Alive and well and in his motorcycle jacket. He was touching one forefinger to the other just the way he had when he'd scared that little boy.

Will did a double take.

The Heart has never given me directions before, she realised. But I think it's telling me to do something.

"I've seen that before," she said aloud. "It means the Heart is telling me to . . . what?" The word was on the tip of her tongue. But she couldn't explain until . . .

Tridart lunged toward Cornelia, his hatchet swinging. Cornelia had him under control for the moment, but she jolted Will back to reality. "Will!" she shouted. "Are you going to help me out here?"

"Of course," cried Will, answering the Heart's question and Cornelia's in the same brief sentence. "Transporting!" That was how they could solve this sticky situation.

Will took a deep breath and tried to clear her mind. She didn't want to drop the Heart.

Back on the bus, Caleb had pointed to

where he'd wanted Boyd to go. But Will didn't need to point. She wanted them right here, in front of her in the woods. Her three missing friends, transported from wherever they were.

Will put a gentle pressure on the Heart, and to her relief it gave way. For a fraction of a second, she extinguished its light.

Then three new beams penetrated the dark of the forest. They hung in the air for the blink of an eye before they disintegrated.

Where the beams had been, three figures materialised. They looked confused and bleary-eyed. They couldn't see in the forest. But they were all there – Hay Lin, Irma, and Taranee. W.I.T.C.H. was ready to take Nerissa on!